ON THE CASE with
HOLMES and WATSON

SHERLOCK HOLMES
and the Adventure of the Dancing Men

Based on the stories of
Sir Arthur Conan Doyle

Adapted by **Murray Shaw** and **M. J. Cosson**
Illustrated by **Sophie Rohrbach**

GRAPHIC UNIVERSE™ · MINNEAPOLIS · NEW YORK · LONDON

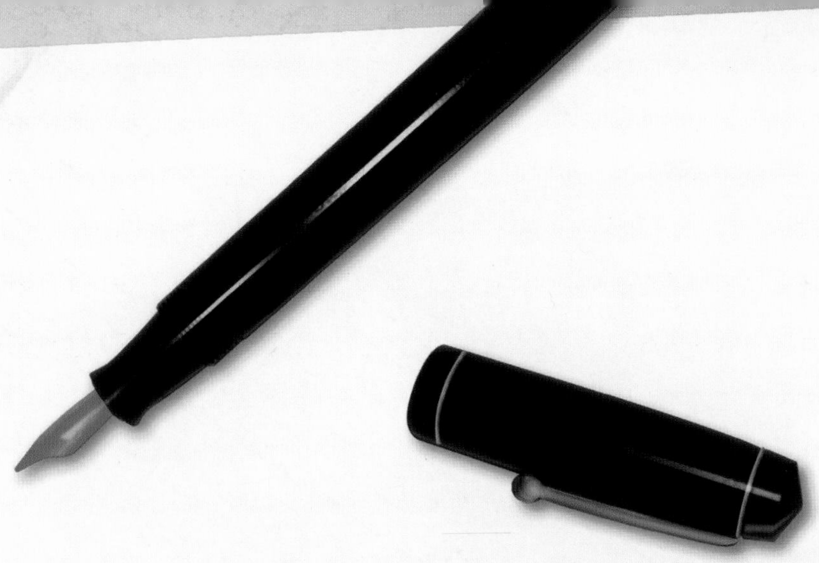

Grateful acknowledgment to Dame Jean Conan Doyle for permission to use the
Sherlock Holmes characters created by Sir Arthur Conan Doyle

Text copyright © 2011 by Murray Shaw
Illustrations © 2011 by Lerner Publishing Group, Inc.

Graphic Universe™ is a trademark of Lerner Publishing Group, Inc.

Graphic Universe™
A division of Lerner Publishing Group, Inc.
241 First Avenue North
Minneapolis, MN 55401 U.S.A.

Website address: www.lernerbooks.com

Library of Congress Cataloging-in-Publication Data

Shaw, Murray.
    #4 Sherlock Holmes and the adventure of the dancing men / adapted by
Murray Shaw and M.J. Cosson ; illustrated by Sophie Rohrbach ; from the
original stories by Sir Arthur Conan Doyle.
        p.   cm. — (On the case with Holmes and Watson)
    Summary: Retold in graphic novel form, Sherlock Holmes investigates
the appearance of some strange drawings. Includes a section explaining
Holmes's reasoning and the clues he used to solve the mystery.
    ISBN: 978-0-7613-6188-6 (lib. bdg. : alk. paper)
    I. Graphic novels. (1. Graphic novels. 2. Doyle, Arthur Conan, Sir, 1859-
1930. Adventure of the dancing men—Adaptations. 3. Mystery and detective
stories.) I. Cosson, M. J. II. Rohrbach, Sophie, ill. III. Doyle, Arthur
Conan, Sir, 1859-1930. Adventure of the dancing men. IV. Title. V. Title:
Adventure of the dancing men.
    PZ7.7.S46Shk 2011   2009051760
    741.5'973—dc22

Manufactured in the United States of America
2—BC—2/1/11

The Story of
SHERLOCK HOLMES
The Famous Detective

Sherlock Holmes and his helpful friend Dr. John Watson are fictional characters created by British writer Sir Arthur Conan Doyle. Doyle published his first novel about the pair, *A Study in Scarlet*, in 1887, and it became very successful. Doyle went on to write fifty-six short stories, as well as three more novels about Holmes's adventures—*The Sign of Four* (1890), *The Hound of the Baskervilles* (1902), and *The Valley of Fear* (1915).

Sherlock Holmes and Dr. Watson have become some of the most famous book characters of all time. Holmes spent most of his time solving mysteries, but he also had a wide array of hobbies, such as playing the violin, boxing, and sword fighting. Watson, a retired army doctor, met Holmes through a mutual friend when Holmes was looking for a roommate. Watson lived with Holmes for several years at 221B Baker Street before marrying and moving out. However, after his marriage, Watson continued to assist Holmes with his cases.

The original versions of the Sherlock Holmes stories are still printed, and many have been made into movies and television shows. Readers continue to be impressed by Holmes's detective methods of observation and scientific reason.

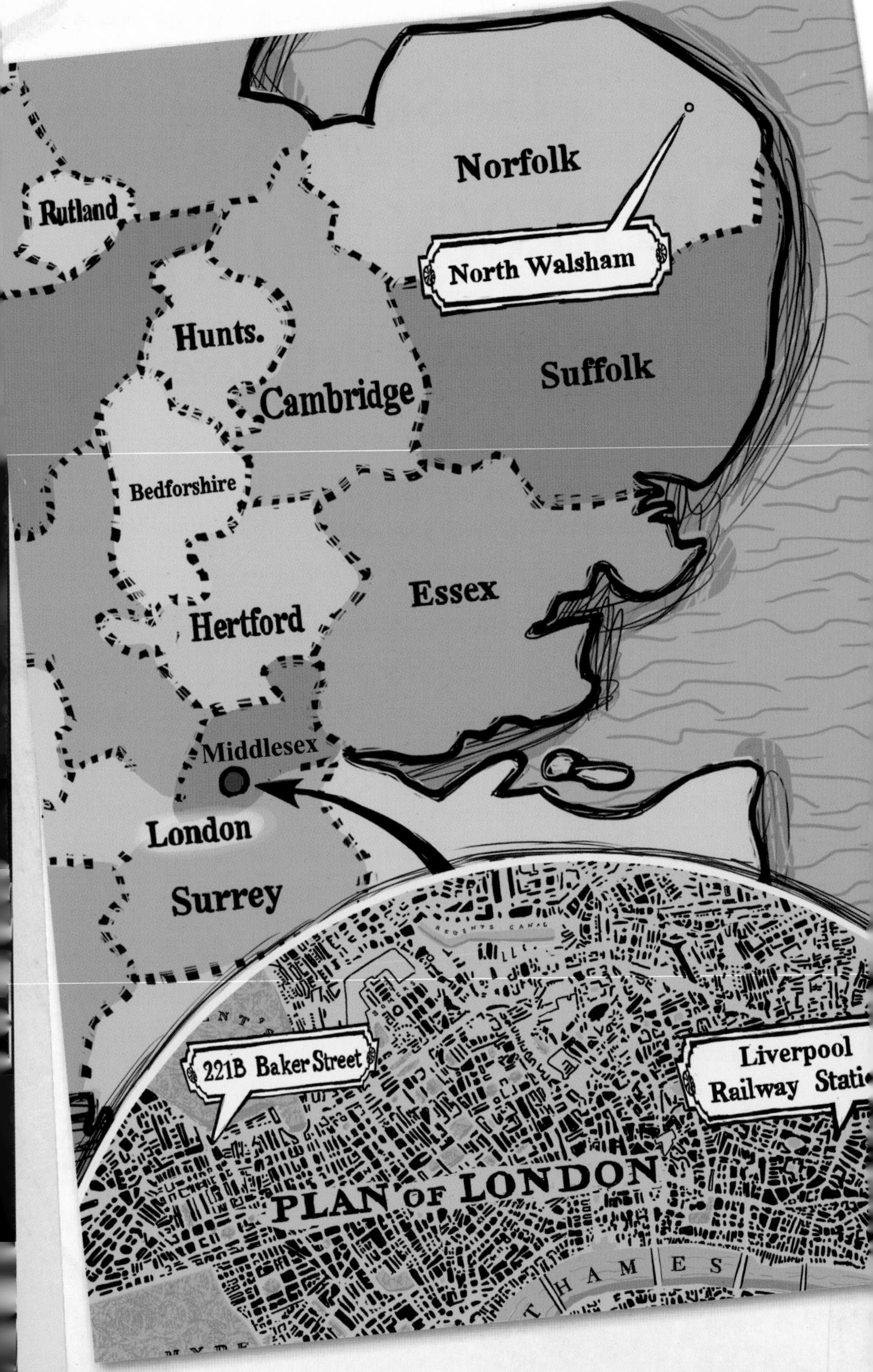
Norfolk
Rutland
North Walsham
Hunts.
Suffolk
Cambridge
Bedforshire
Essex
Hertford
Middlesex
London
Surrey
REGENTS CANAL
221B Baker Street
Liverpool
Railway Stati
PLAN OF LONDON
THAMES

Character List

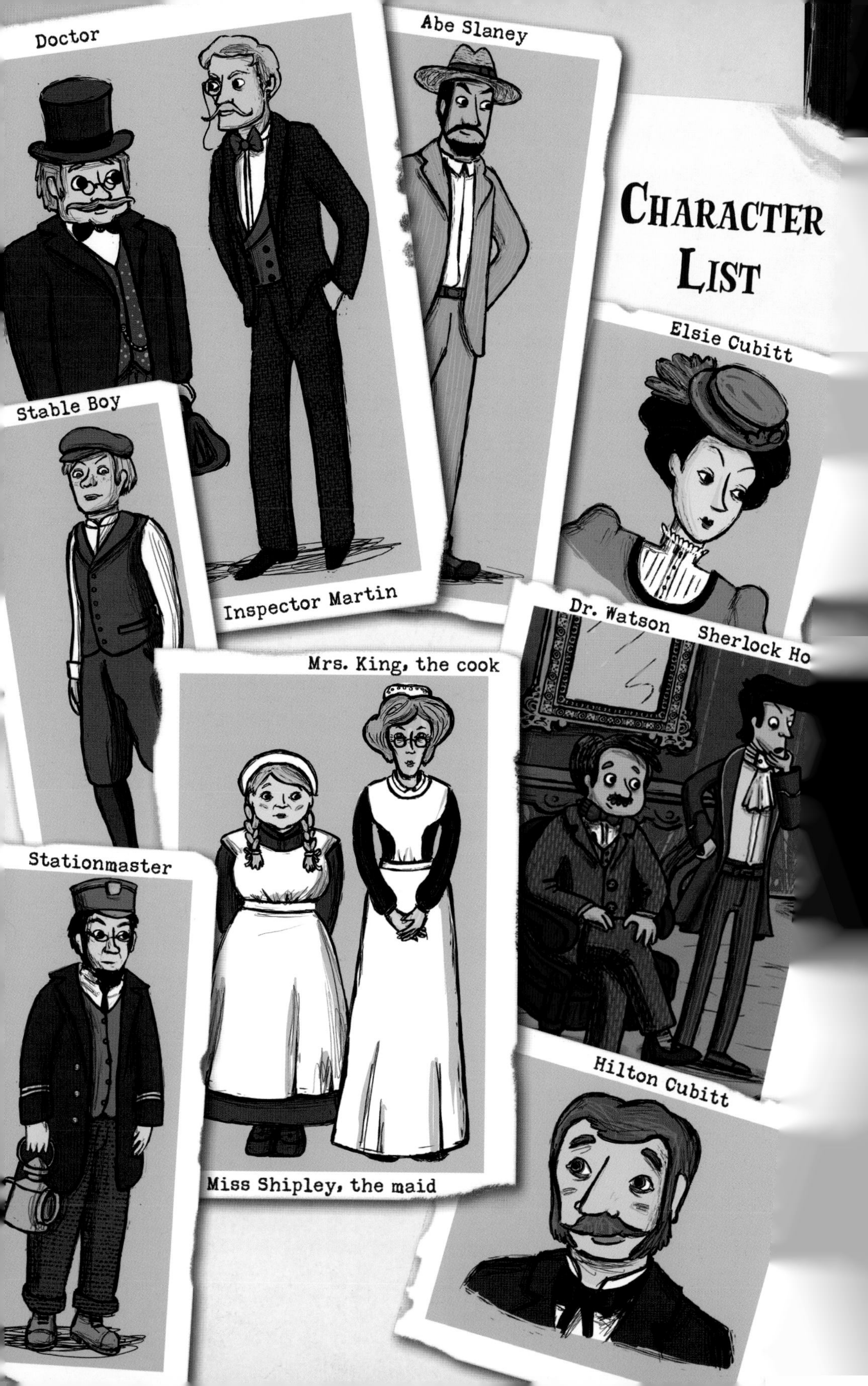
Doctor
Abe Slaney
Stable Boy
Inspector Martin
Elsie Cubitt
Dr. Watson
Sherlock Ho
Mrs. King, the cook
Stationmaster
Miss Shipley, the maid
Hilton Cubitt

From the Desk of
John H. Watson, M.D.

My name is Dr. John H. Watson. For several years, I have been assisting my friend, Sherlock Holmes, in solving mysteries throughout the bustling city of London and beyond. Holmes is a peculiar man—always questioning and reasoning his way through various problems. But when I first met him in 1878, I was immediately intrigued by his oddities.

Holmes has always been more daring than I, and his logical deduction never ceases to amaze me. I have begun writing down all of the adventures I have with Holmes. This is one of those stories.

Sincerely,

Dr. Watson

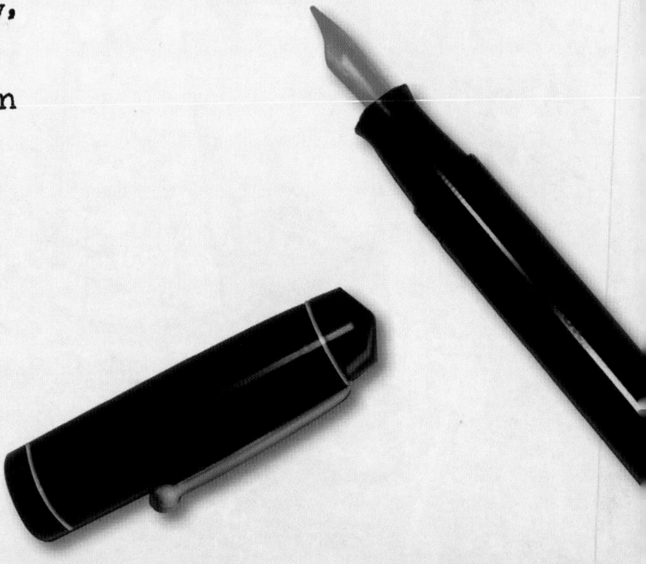

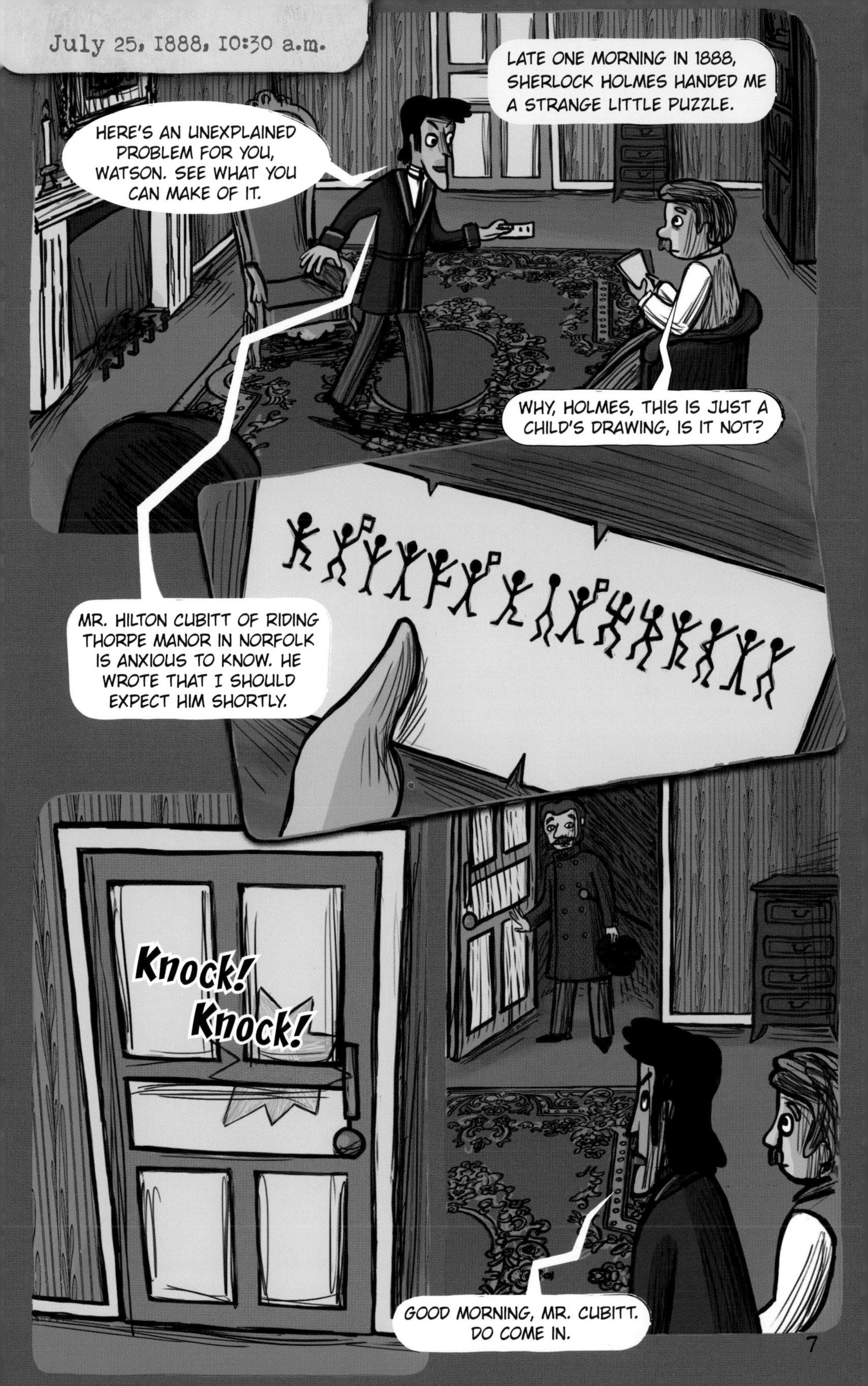
July 25, 1888, 10:30 a.m.
LATE ONE MORNING IN 1888, SHERLOCK HOLMES HANDED ME A STRANGE LITTLE PUZZLE.
HERE'S AN UNEXPLAINED PROBLEM FOR YOU, WATSON. SEE WHAT YOU CAN MAKE OF IT.
WHY, HOLMES, THIS IS JUST A CHILD'S DRAWING, IS IT NOT?
MR. HILTON CUBITT OF RIDING THORPE MANOR IN NORFOLK IS ANXIOUS TO KNOW. HE WROTE THAT I SHOULD EXPECT HIM SHORTLY.
Knock! Knock!
GOOD MORNING, MR. CUBITT. DO COME IN.

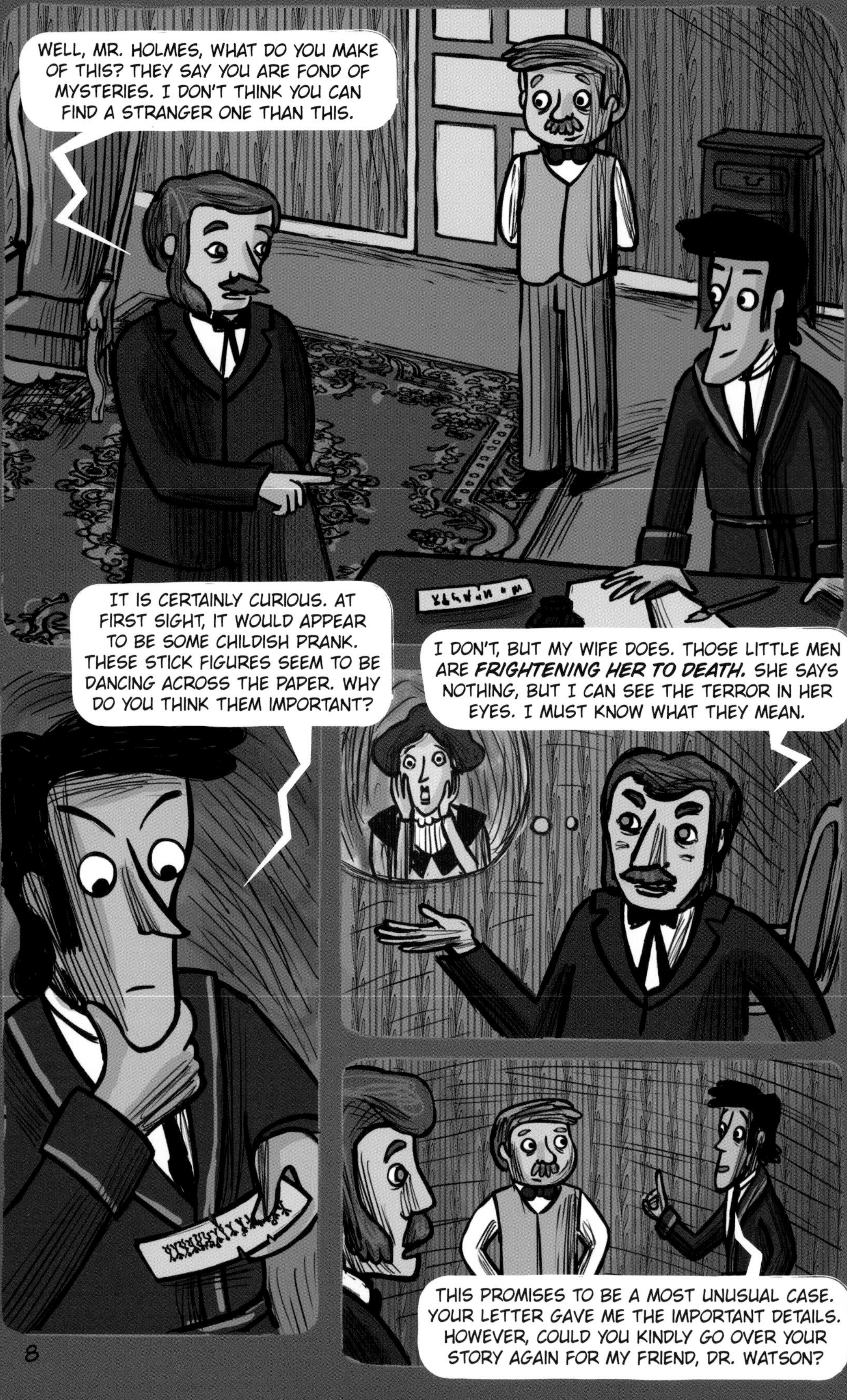
WELL, MR. HOLMES, WHAT DO YOU MAKE OF THIS? THEY SAY YOU ARE FOND OF MYSTERIES. I DON'T THINK YOU CAN FIND A STRANGER ONE THAN THIS.
IT IS CERTAINLY CURIOUS. AT FIRST SIGHT, IT WOULD APPEAR TO BE SOME CHILDISH PRANK. THESE STICK FIGURES SEEM TO BE DANCING ACROSS THE PAPER. WHY DO YOU THINK THEM IMPORTANT?
I DON'T, BUT MY WIFE DOES. THOSE LITTLE MEN ARE ***FRIGHTENING HER TO DEATH.*** SHE SAYS NOTHING, BUT I CAN SEE THE TERROR IN HER EYES. I MUST KNOW WHAT THEY MEAN.
THIS PROMISES TO BE A MOST UNUSUAL CASE. YOUR LETTER GAVE ME THE IMPORTANT DETAILS. HOWEVER, COULD YOU KINDLY GO OVER YOUR STORY AGAIN FOR MY FRIEND, DR. WATSON?

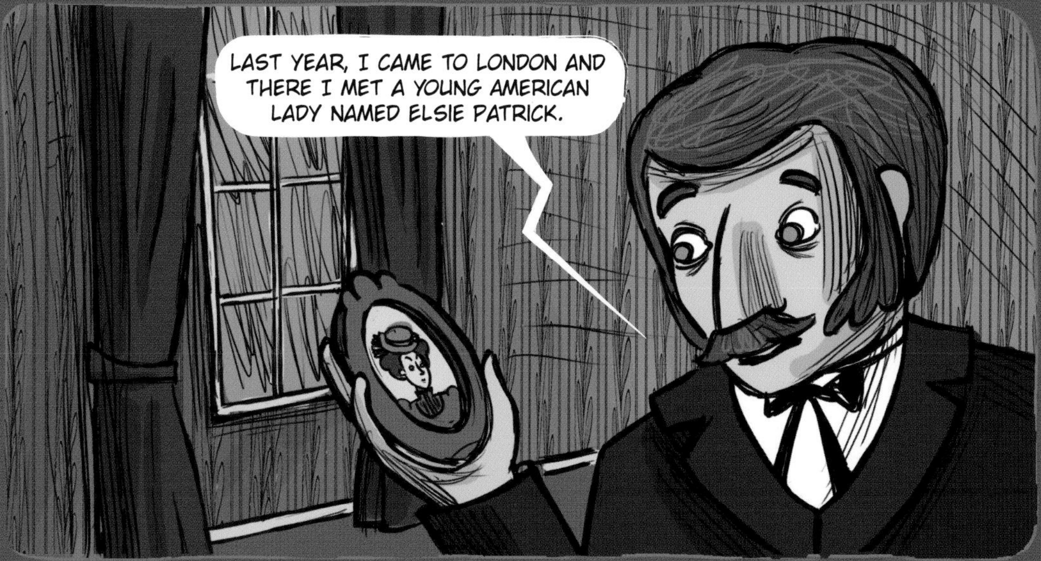
LAST YEAR, I CAME TO LONDON AND THERE I MET A YOUNG AMERICAN LADY NAMED ELSIE PATRICK.

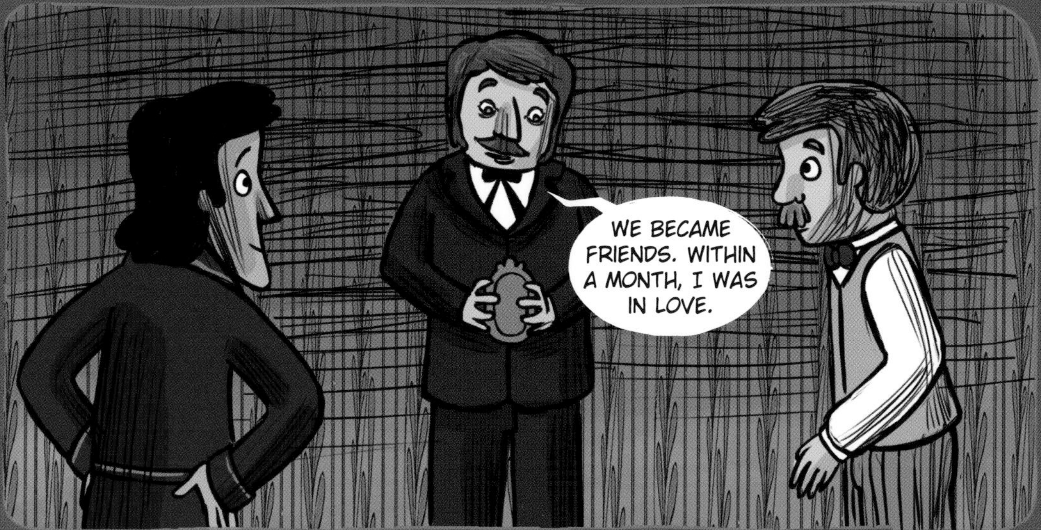
WE BECAME FRIENDS. WITHIN A MONTH, I WAS IN LOVE.

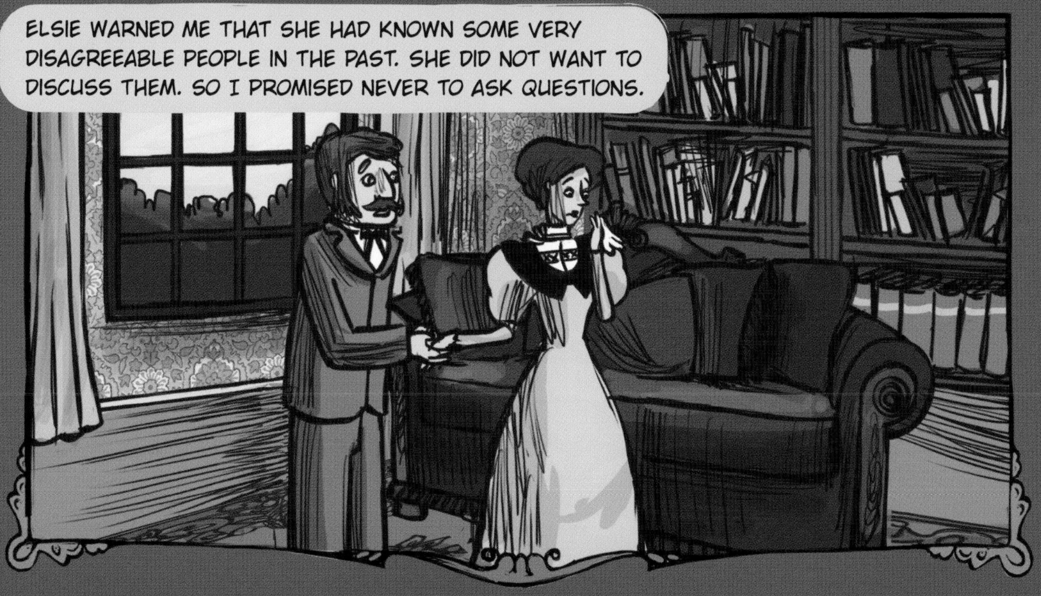
ELSIE WARNED ME THAT SHE HAD KNOWN SOME VERY DISAGREEABLE PEOPLE IN THE PAST. SHE DID NOT WANT TO DISCUSS THEM. SO I PROMISED NEVER TO ASK QUESTIONS.

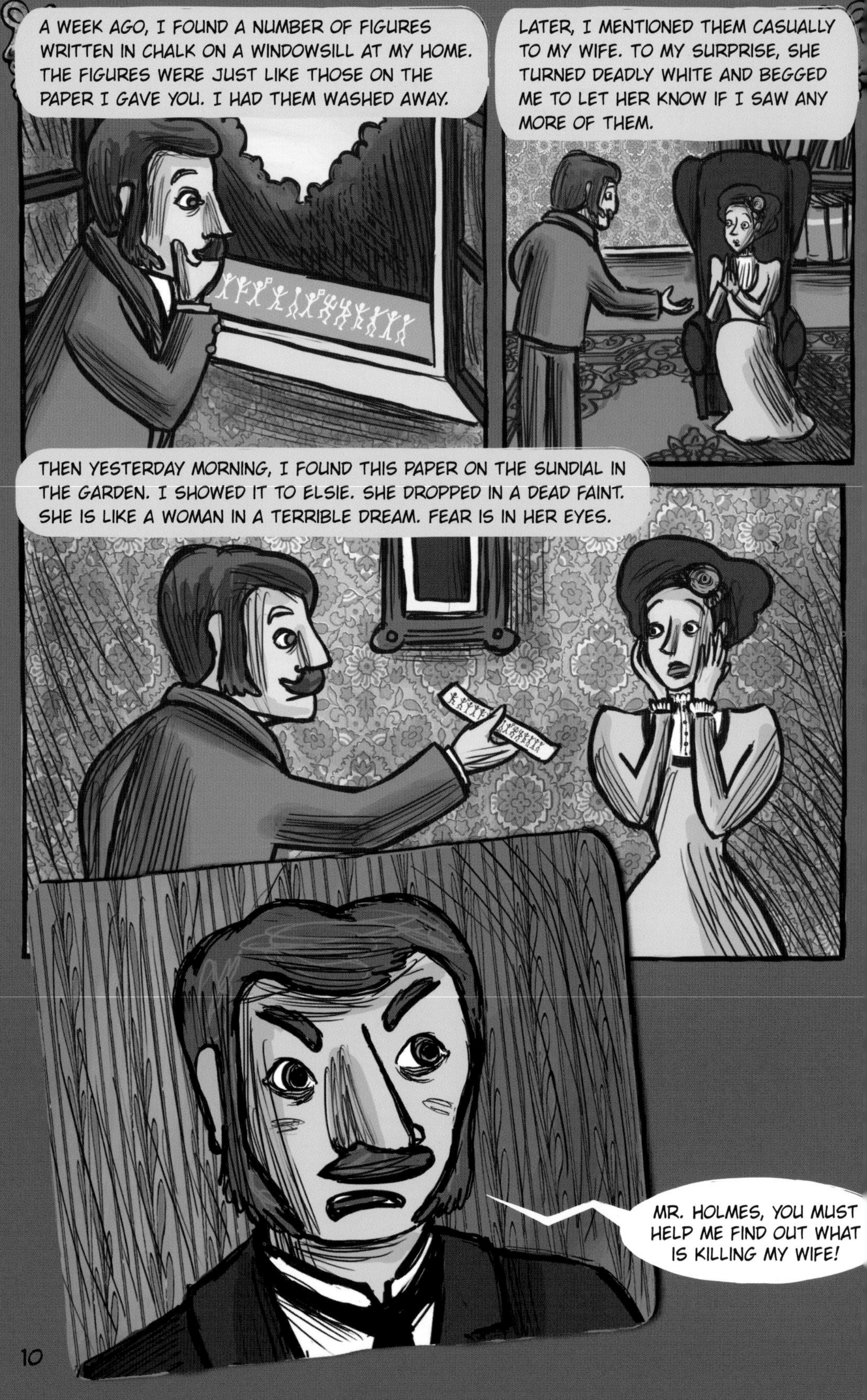
A WEEK AGO, I FOUND A NUMBER OF FIGURES WRITTEN IN CHALK ON A WINDOWSILL AT MY HOME. THE FIGURES WERE JUST LIKE THOSE ON THE PAPER I GAVE YOU. I HAD THEM WASHED AWAY.
LATER, I MENTIONED THEM CASUALLY TO MY WIFE. TO MY SURPRISE, SHE TURNED DEADLY WHITE AND BEGGED ME TO LET HER KNOW IF I SAW ANY MORE OF THEM.
THEN YESTERDAY MORNING, I FOUND THIS PAPER ON THE SUNDIAL IN THE GARDEN. I SHOWED IT TO ELSIE. SHE DROPPED IN A DEAD FAINT. SHE IS LIKE A WOMAN IN A TERRIBLE DREAM. FEAR IS IN HER EYES.
MR. HOLMES, YOU MUST HELP ME FIND OUT WHAT IS KILLING MY WIFE!

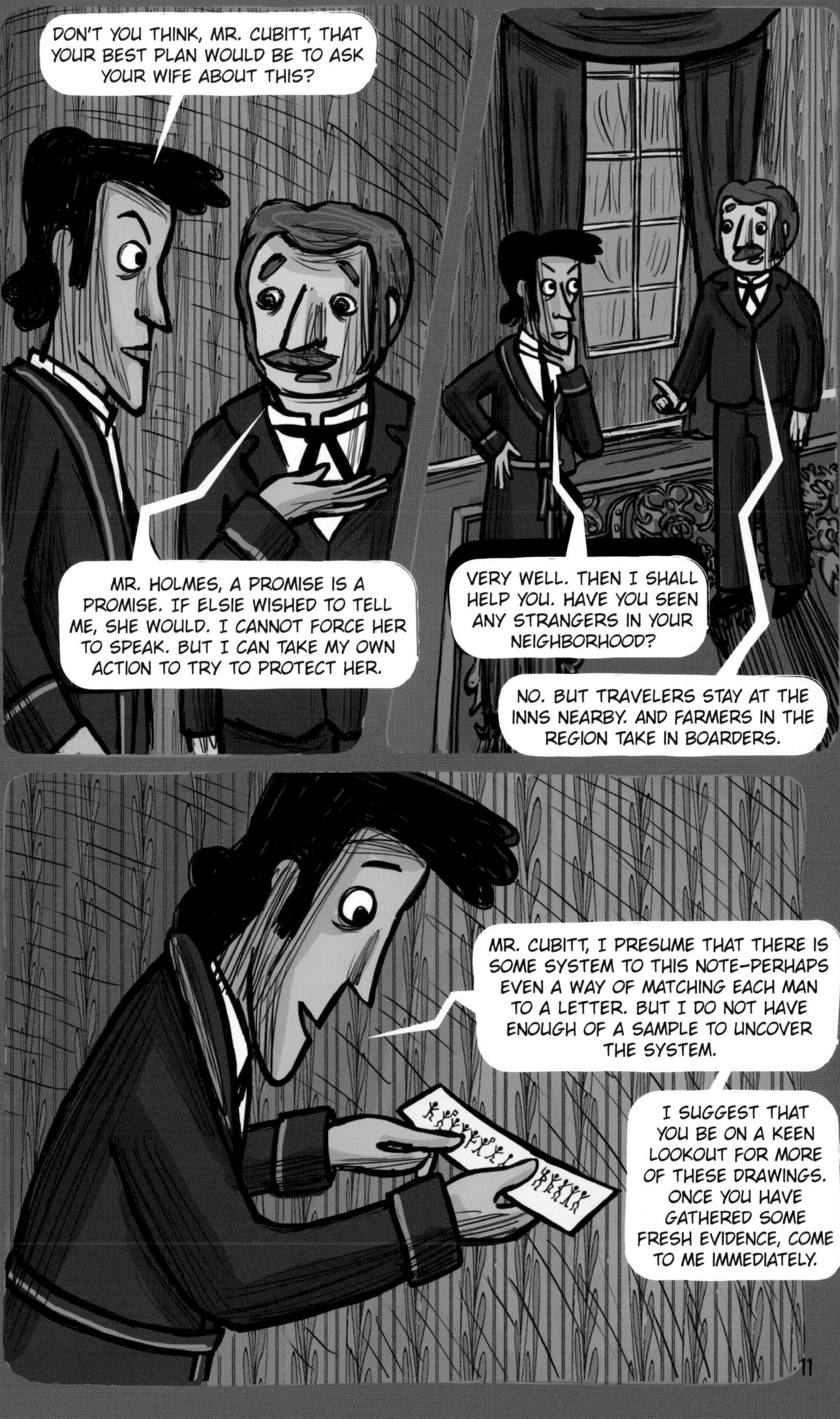
DON'T YOU THINK, MR. CUBITT, THAT YOUR BEST PLAN WOULD BE TO ASK YOUR WIFE ABOUT THIS?
MR. HOLMES, A PROMISE IS A PROMISE. IF ELSIE WISHED TO TELL ME, SHE WOULD. I CANNOT FORCE HER TO SPEAK. BUT I CAN TAKE MY OWN ACTION TO TRY TO PROTECT HER.
VERY WELL. THEN I SHALL HELP YOU. HAVE YOU SEEN ANY STRANGERS IN YOUR NEIGHBORHOOD?
NO. BUT TRAVELERS STAY AT THE INNS NEARBY. AND FARMERS IN THE REGION TAKE IN BOARDERS.
MR. CUBITT, I PRESUME THAT THERE IS SOME SYSTEM TO THIS NOTE—PERHAPS EVEN A WAY OF MATCHING EACH MAN TO A LETTER. BUT I DO NOT HAVE ENOUGH OF A SAMPLE TO UNCOVER THE SYSTEM.
I SUGGEST THAT YOU BE ON A KEEN LOOKOUT FOR MORE OF THESE DRAWINGS. ONCE YOU HAVE GATHERED SOME FRESH EVIDENCE, COME TO ME IMMEDIATELY.

The visit left Holmes in a thoughtful mood. From time to time, I saw him look long and earnestly at the slip of paper. He did not speak of the matter, however, until one afternoon two weeks later. I was just going out when he called me back to tell me that Hilton Cubitt would be arriving at any moment. It seems there had been some new incidents. We hadn't long to wait.

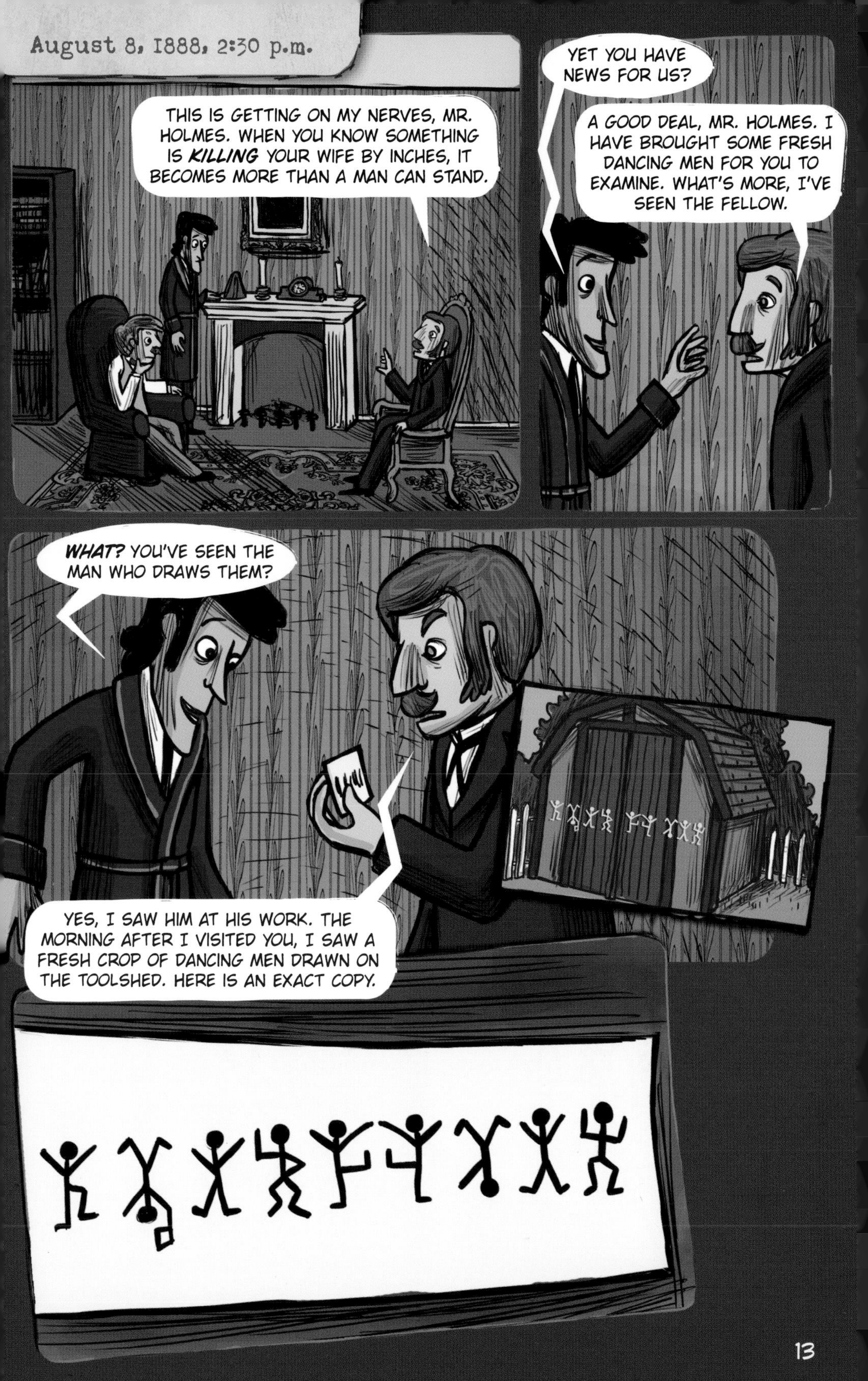
August 8, 1888, 2:30 p.m.
THIS IS GETTING ON MY NERVES, MR. HOLMES. WHEN YOU KNOW SOMETHING IS KILLING YOUR WIFE BY INCHES, IT BECOMES MORE THAN A MAN CAN STAND.
YET YOU HAVE NEWS FOR US?
A GOOD DEAL, MR. HOLMES. I HAVE BROUGHT SOME FRESH DANCING MEN FOR YOU TO EXAMINE. WHAT'S MORE, I'VE SEEN THE FELLOW.
WHAT? YOU'VE SEEN THE MAN WHO DRAWS THEM?
YES, I SAW HIM AT HIS WORK. THE MORNING AFTER I VISITED YOU, I SAW A FRESH CROP OF DANCING MEN DRAWN ON THE TOOLSHED. HERE IS AN EXACT COPY.

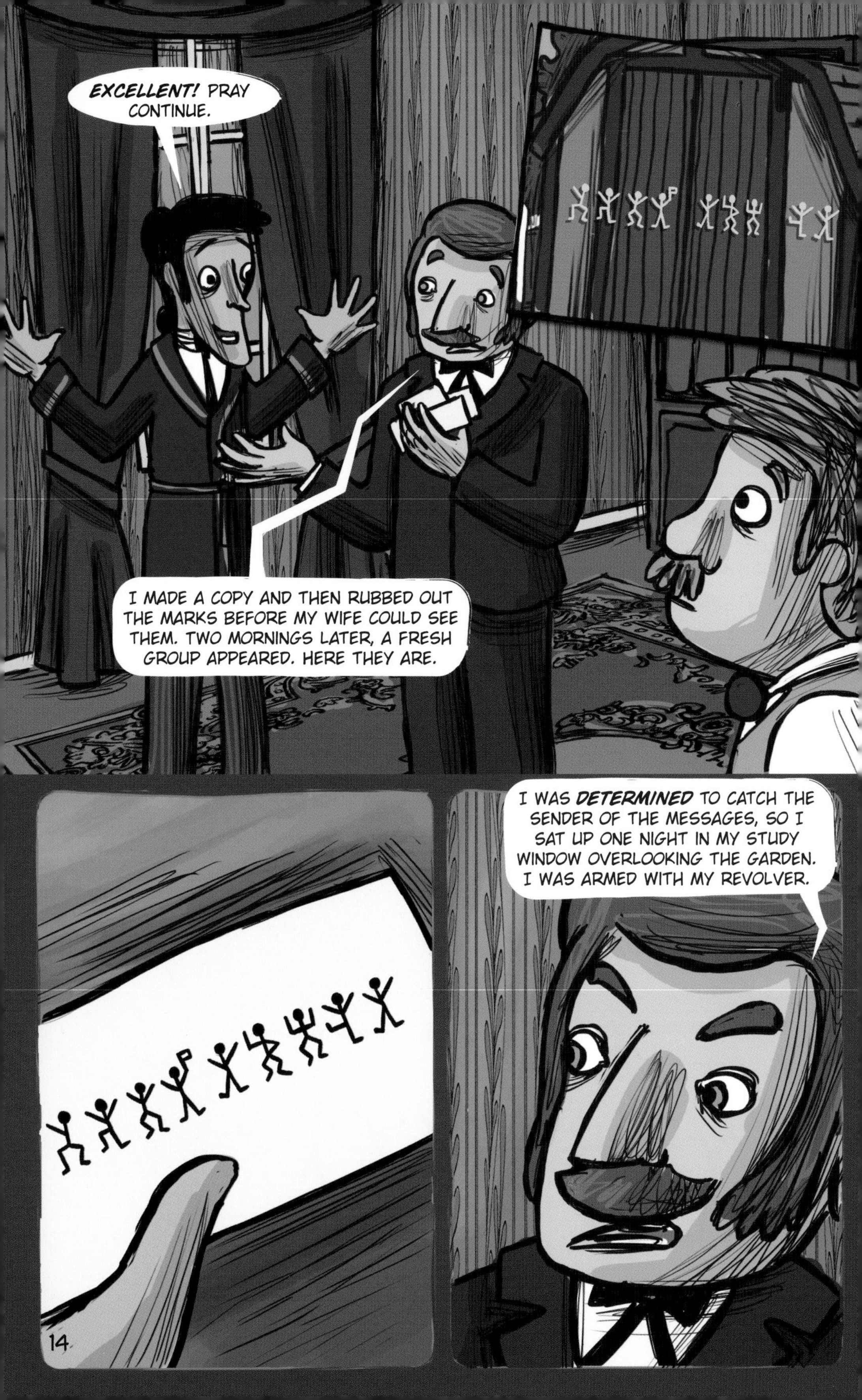
EXCELLENT! PRAY CONTINUE.
I MADE A COPY AND THEN RUBBED OUT THE MARKS BEFORE MY WIFE COULD SEE THEM. TWO MORNINGS LATER, A FRESH GROUP APPEARED. HERE THEY ARE.
I WAS DETERMINED TO CATCH THE SENDER OF THE MESSAGES, SO I SAT UP ONE NIGHT IN MY STUDY WINDOW OVERLOOKING THE GARDEN. I WAS ARMED WITH MY REVOLVER.

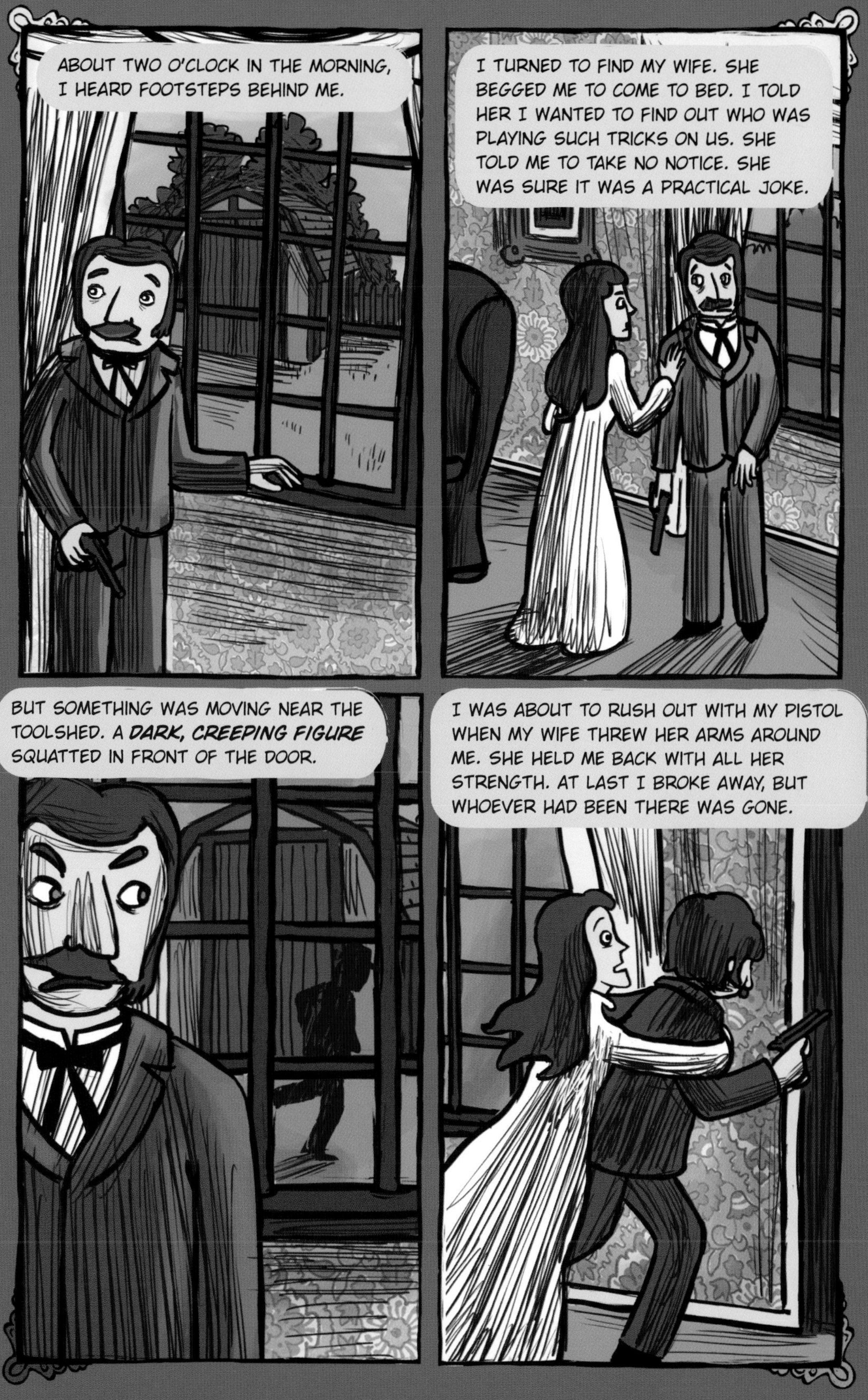
ABOUT TWO O'CLOCK IN THE MORNING, I HEARD FOOTSTEPS BEHIND ME.
I TURNED TO FIND MY WIFE. SHE BEGGED ME TO COME TO BED. I TOLD HER I WANTED TO FIND OUT WHO WAS PLAYING SUCH TRICKS ON US. SHE TOLD ME TO TAKE NO NOTICE. SHE WAS SURE IT WAS A PRACTICAL JOKE.
BUT SOMETHING WAS MOVING NEAR THE TOOLSHED. A ***DARK, CREEPING FIGURE*** SQUATTED IN FRONT OF THE DOOR.
I WAS ABOUT TO RUSH OUT WITH MY PISTOL WHEN MY WIFE THREW HER ARMS AROUND ME. SHE HELD ME BACK WITH ALL HER STRENGTH. AT LAST I BROKE AWAY, BUT WHOEVER HAD BEEN THERE WAS GONE.

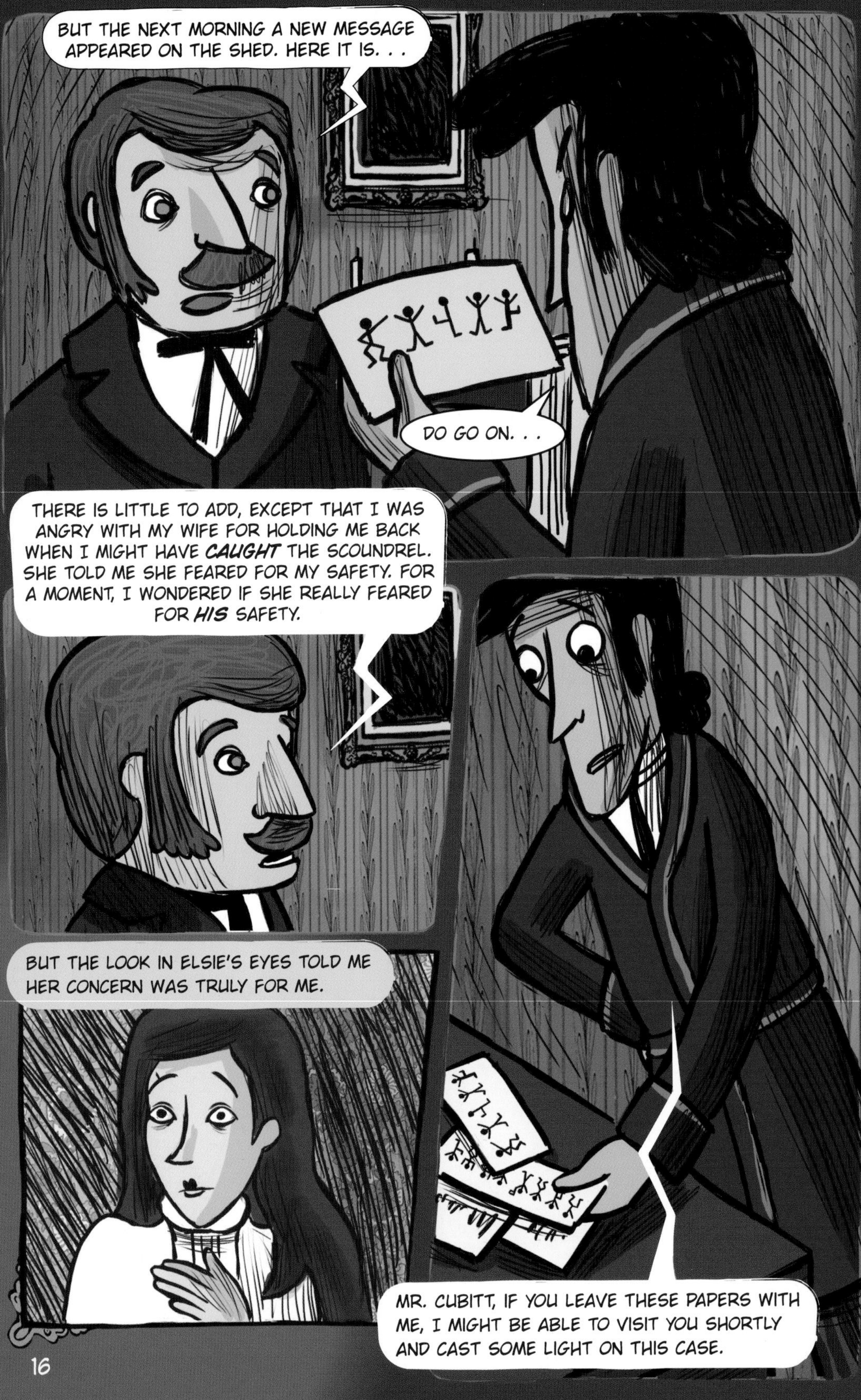
BUT THE NEXT MORNING A NEW MESSAGE APPEARED ON THE SHED. HERE IT IS. . .
DO GO ON. . .
THERE IS LITTLE TO ADD, EXCEPT THAT I WAS ANGRY WITH MY WIFE FOR HOLDING ME BACK WHEN I MIGHT HAVE *CAUGHT* THE SCOUNDREL. SHE TOLD ME SHE FEARED FOR MY SAFETY. FOR A MOMENT, I WONDERED IF SHE REALLY FEARED FOR *HIS* SAFETY.
BUT THE LOOK IN ELSIE'S EYES TOLD ME HER CONCERN WAS TRULY FOR ME.
MR. CUBITT, IF YOU LEAVE THESE PAPERS WITH ME, I MIGHT BE ABLE TO VISIT YOU SHORTLY AND CAST SOME LIGHT ON THIS CASE.

Cubitt thanked us both heartily and turned to go. The moment his back had passed through the door, Holmes put out on the table all the slips of paper. Then he threw himself into trying to make sense of the dancing figures. He covered sheet after sheet of paper with figures and letters. He was so absorbed in his task that he had evidently forgotten my presence. At times he scowled at his work, and at other times, he began to whistle.

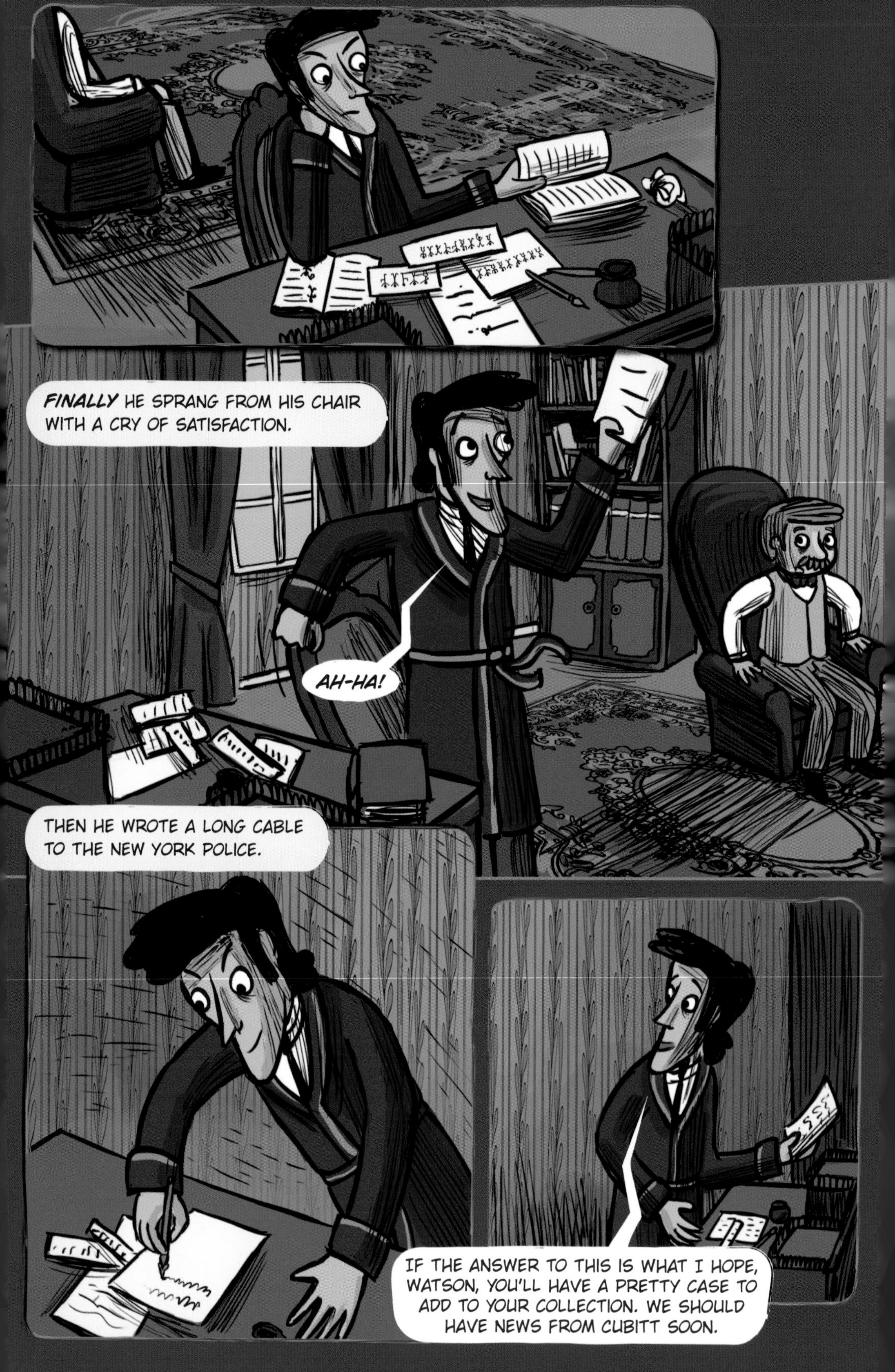
FINALLY HE SPRANG FROM HIS CHAIR WITH A CRY OF SATISFACTION.
AH-HA!
THEN HE WROTE A LONG CABLE TO THE NEW YORK POLICE.
IF THE ANSWER TO THIS IS WHAT I HOPE, WATSON, YOU'LL HAVE A PRETTY CASE TO ADD TO YOUR COLLECTION. WE SHOULD HAVE NEWS FROM CUBITT SOON.

August 10, 1888, 7:00 p.m.

But two days passed, and no response to the cable arrived. Each time the bell rang, Holmes jumped up with expectation. Finally, on the evening of the second day, the New York police responded to Holmes's message and a letter arrived from Mr. Cubitt. All was quiet, Cubitt wrote, but a long drawing had appeared on the sundial. He enclosed a copy of it.

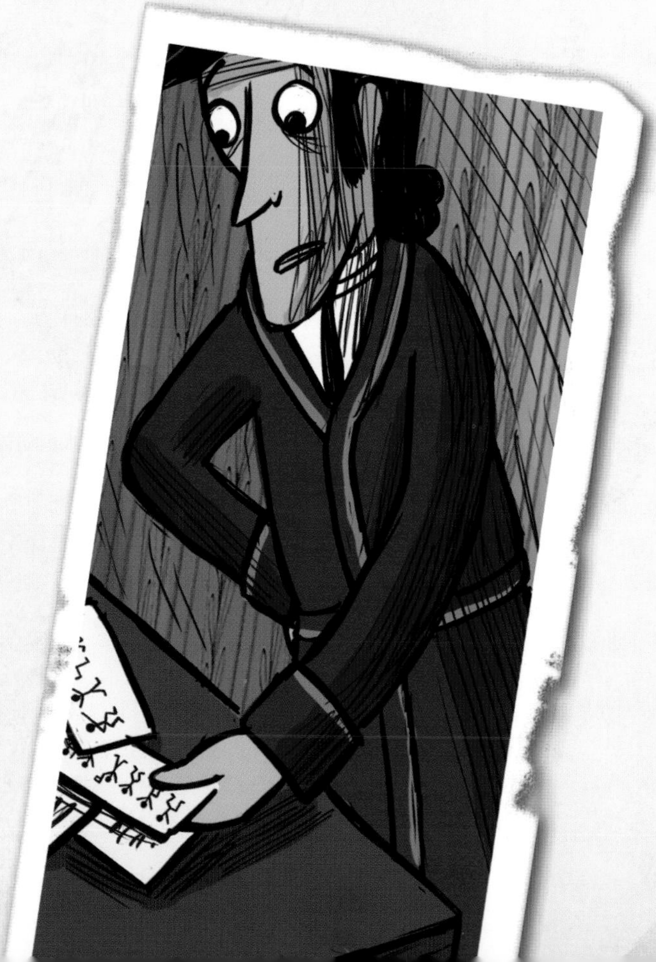

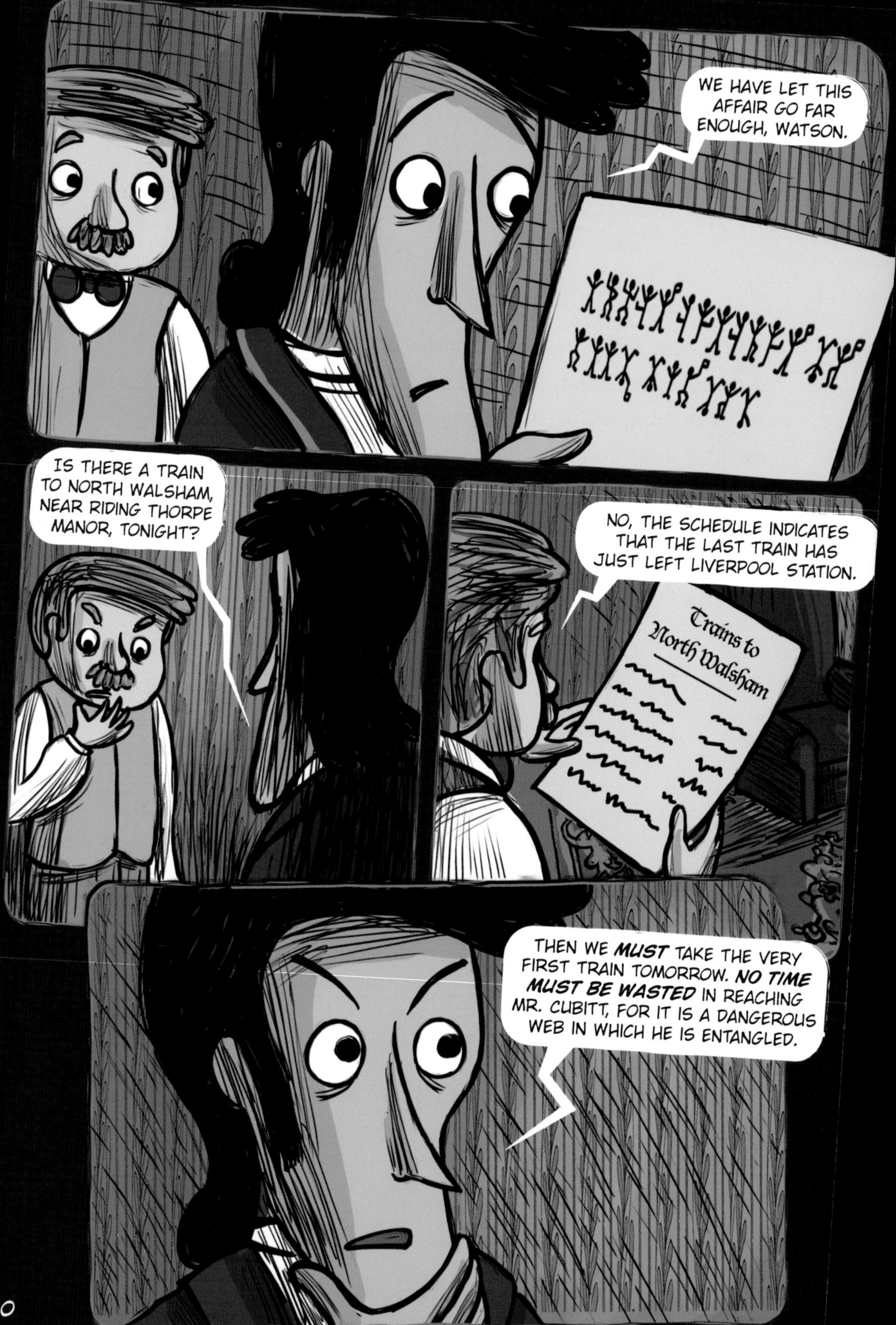
WE HAVE LET THIS AFFAIR GO FAR ENOUGH, WATSON.
IS THERE A TRAIN TO NORTH WALSHAM, NEAR RIDING THORPE MANOR, TONIGHT?
NO, THE SCHEDULE INDICATES THAT THE LAST TRAIN HAS JUST LEFT LIVERPOOL STATION.
Trains to North Walsham
THEN WE MUST TAKE THE VERY FIRST TRAIN TOMORROW. NO TIME MUST BE WASTED IN REACHING MR. CUBITT, FOR IT IS A DANGEROUS WEB IN WHICH HE IS ENTANGLED.

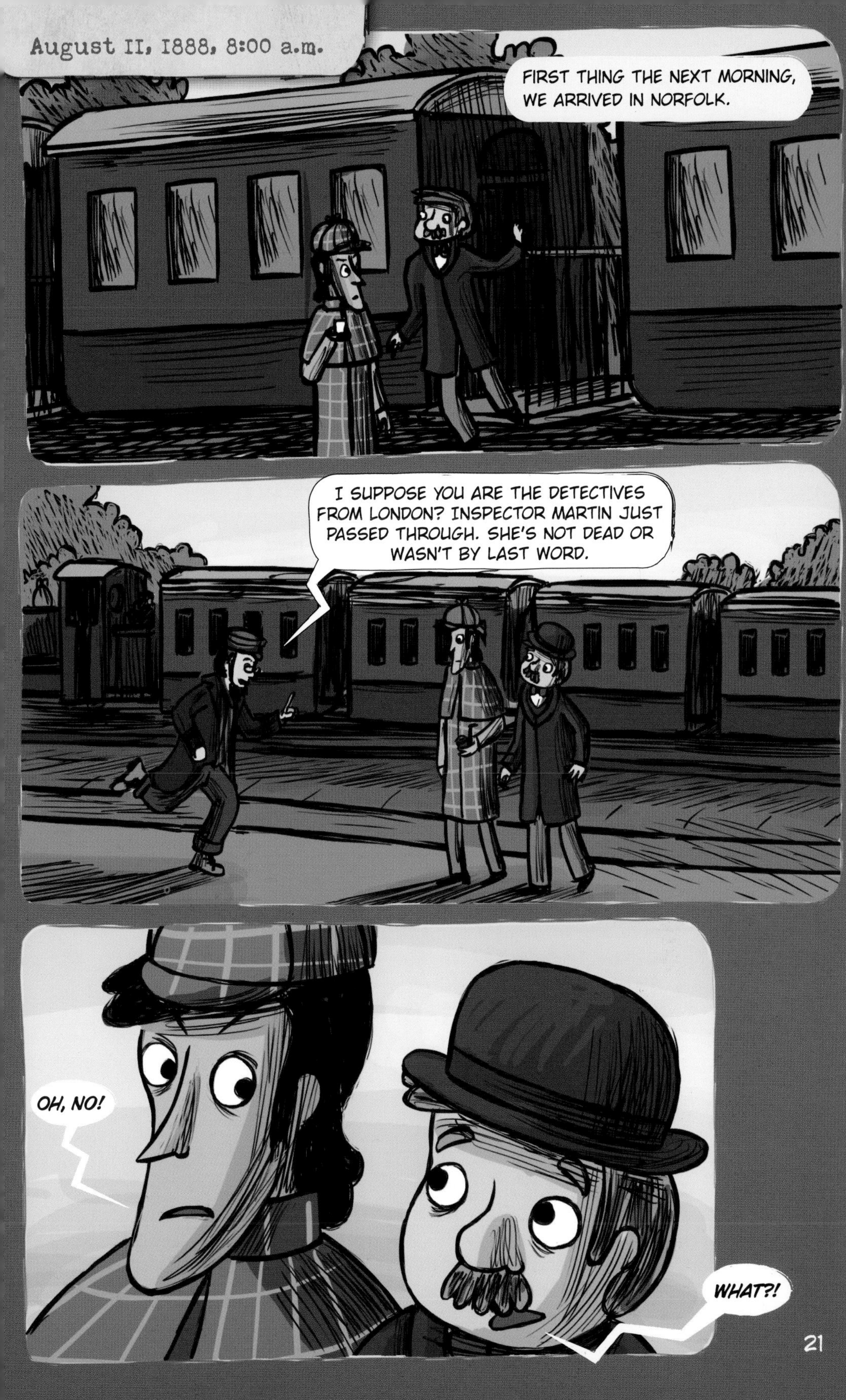

August 11, 1888, 8:00 a.m.
FIRST THING THE NEXT MORNING, WE ARRIVED IN NORFOLK.
I SUPPOSE YOU ARE THE DETECTIVES FROM LONDON? INSPECTOR MARTIN JUST PASSED THROUGH. SHE'S NOT DEAD OR WASN'T BY LAST WORD.
OH, NO!
WHAT?!

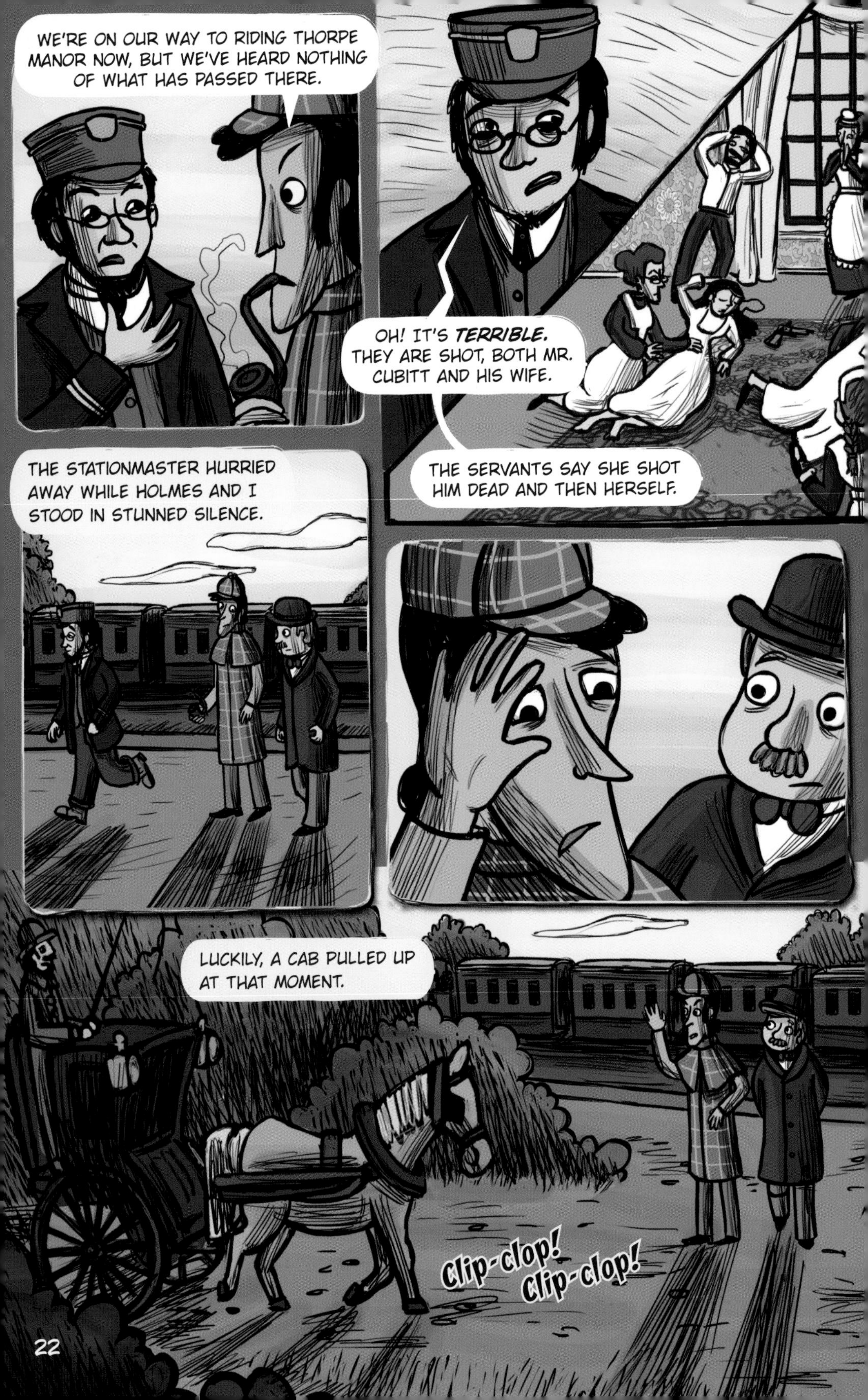
WE'RE ON OUR WAY TO RIDING THORPE MANOR NOW, BUT WE'VE HEARD NOTHING OF WHAT HAS PASSED THERE.
OH! IT'S **TERRIBLE.** THEY ARE SHOT, BOTH MR. CUBITT AND HIS WIFE.
THE SERVANTS SAY SHE SHOT HIM DEAD AND THEN HERSELF.
THE STATIONMASTER HURRIED AWAY WHILE HOLMES AND I STOOD IN STUNNED SILENCE.
LUCKILY, A CAB PULLED UP AT THAT MOMENT.
Clip-clop! Clip-clop!

Holmes headed straight for the cab. Throughout the rest of our journey, he never said a word. Seldom have I seen him so utterly without hope. His worst fears had become real. A black gloom settled upon him.

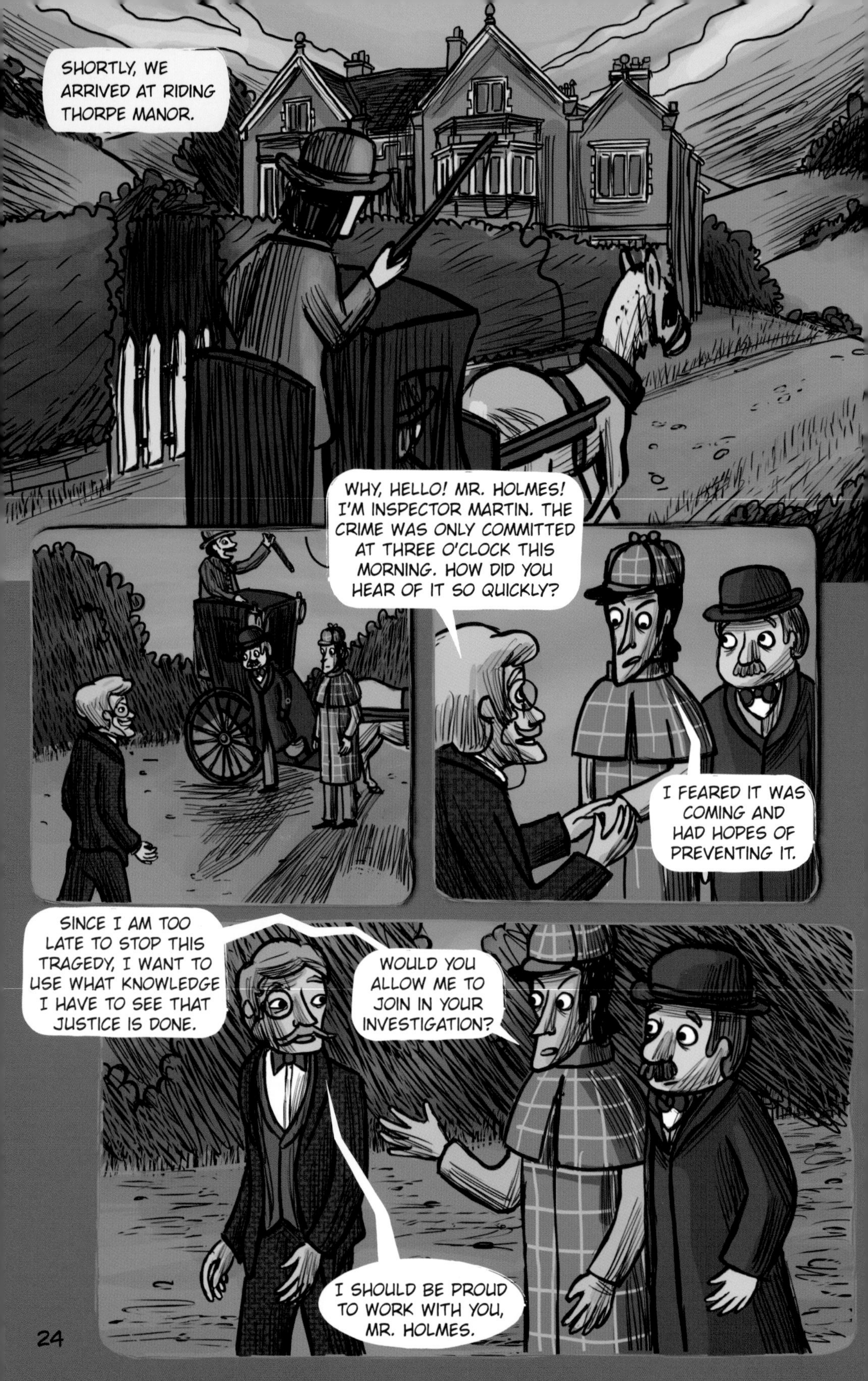
SHORTLY, WE ARRIVED AT RIDING THORPE MANOR.
WHY, HELLO! MR. HOLMES! I'M INSPECTOR MARTIN. THE CRIME WAS ONLY COMMITTED AT THREE O'CLOCK THIS MORNING. HOW DID YOU HEAR OF IT SO QUICKLY?
I FEARED IT WAS COMING AND HAD HOPES OF PREVENTING IT.
SINCE I AM TOO LATE TO STOP THIS TRAGEDY, I WANT TO USE WHAT KNOWLEDGE I HAVE TO SEE THAT JUSTICE IS DONE.
WOULD YOU ALLOW ME TO JOIN IN YOUR INVESTIGATION?
I SHOULD BE PROUD TO WORK WITH YOU, MR. HOLMES.

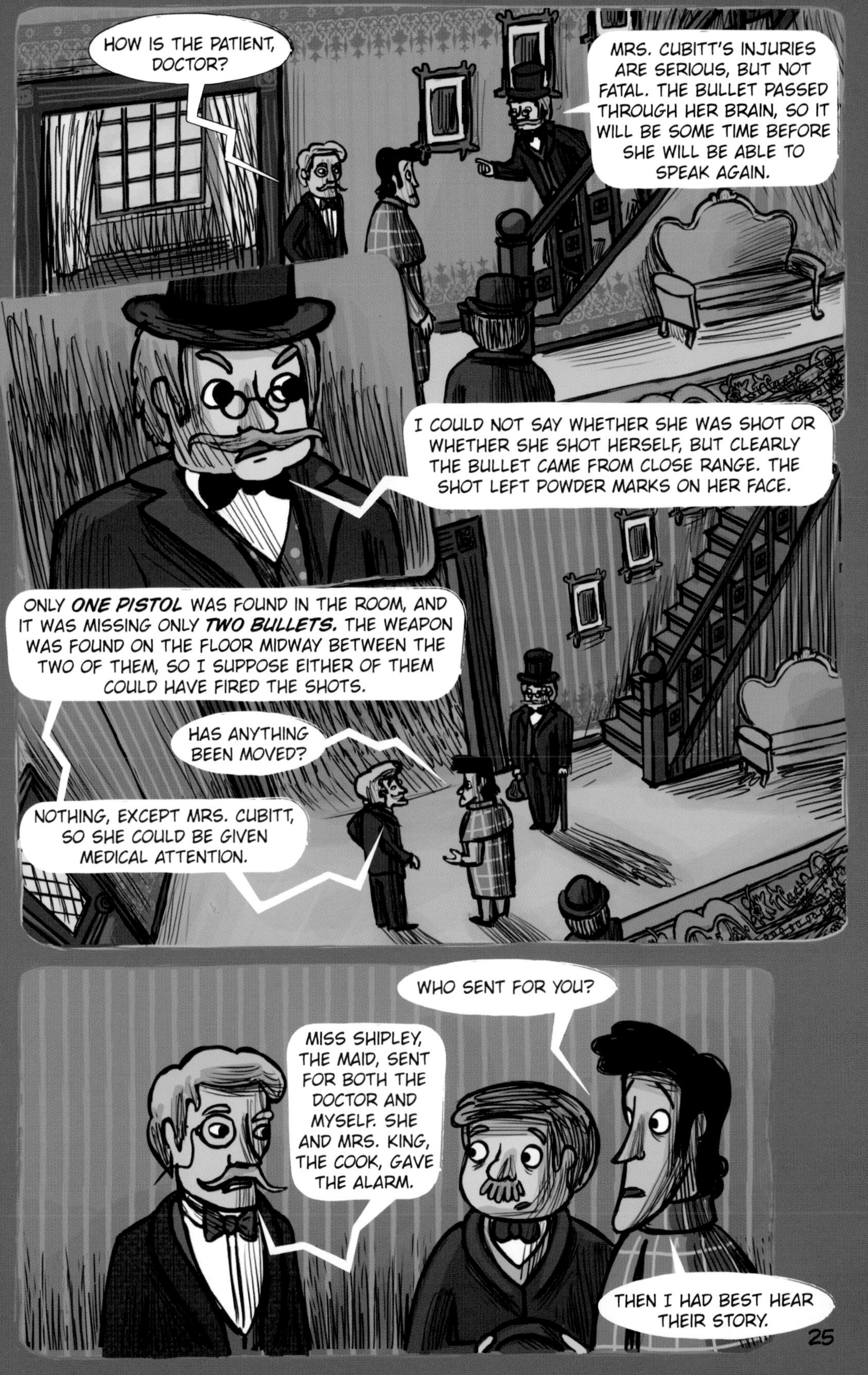
HOW IS THE PATIENT, DOCTOR?
MRS. CUBITT'S INJURIES ARE SERIOUS, BUT NOT FATAL. THE BULLET PASSED THROUGH HER BRAIN, SO IT WILL BE SOME TIME BEFORE SHE WILL BE ABLE TO SPEAK AGAIN.
I COULD NOT SAY WHETHER SHE WAS SHOT OR WHETHER SHE SHOT HERSELF, BUT CLEARLY THE BULLET CAME FROM CLOSE RANGE. THE SHOT LEFT POWDER MARKS ON HER FACE.
ONLY ***ONE PISTOL*** WAS FOUND IN THE ROOM, AND IT WAS MISSING ONLY ***TWO BULLETS.*** THE WEAPON WAS FOUND ON THE FLOOR MIDWAY BETWEEN THE TWO OF THEM, SO I SUPPOSE EITHER OF THEM COULD HAVE FIRED THE SHOTS.
HAS ANYTHING BEEN MOVED?
NOTHING, EXCEPT MRS. CUBITT, SO SHE COULD BE GIVEN MEDICAL ATTENTION.
WHO SENT FOR YOU?
MISS SHIPLEY, THE MAID, SENT FOR BOTH THE DOCTOR AND MYSELF. SHE AND MRS. KING, THE COOK, GAVE THE ALARM.
THEN I HAD BEST HEAR THEIR STORY.

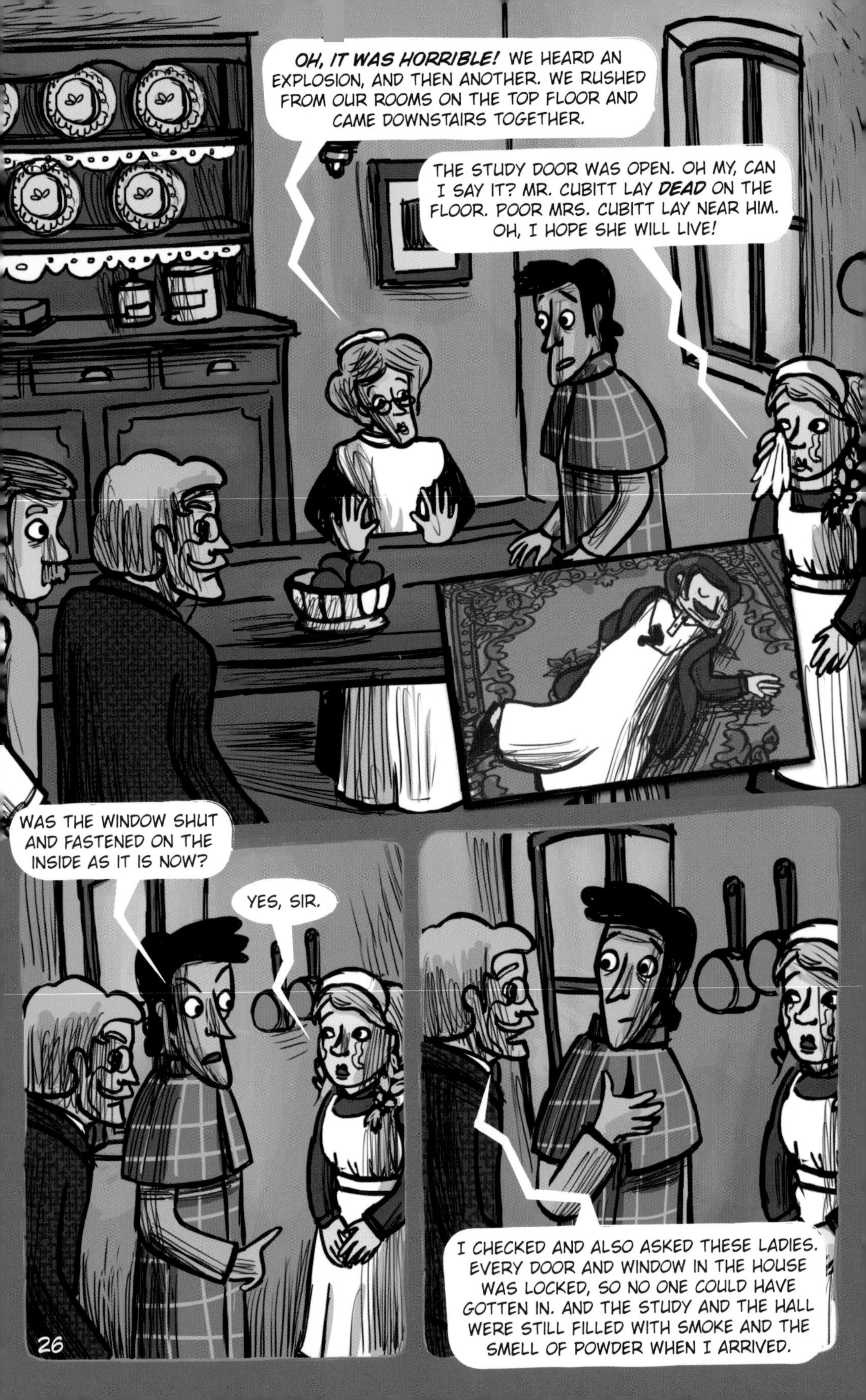

OH, IT WAS HORRIBLE! WE HEARD AN EXPLOSION, AND THEN ANOTHER. WE RUSHED FROM OUR ROOMS ON THE TOP FLOOR AND CAME DOWNSTAIRS TOGETHER.
THE STUDY DOOR WAS OPEN. OH MY, CAN I SAY IT? MR. CUBITT LAY DEAD ON THE FLOOR. POOR MRS. CUBITT LAY NEAR HIM. OH, I HOPE SHE WILL LIVE!
WAS THE WINDOW SHUT AND FASTENED ON THE INSIDE AS IT IS NOW?
YES, SIR.
I CHECKED AND ALSO ASKED THESE LADIES. EVERY DOOR AND WINDOW IN THE HOUSE WAS LOCKED, SO NO ONE COULD HAVE GOTTEN IN. AND THE STUDY AND THE HALL WERE STILL FILLED WITH SMOKE AND THE SMELL OF POWDER WHEN I ARRIVED.

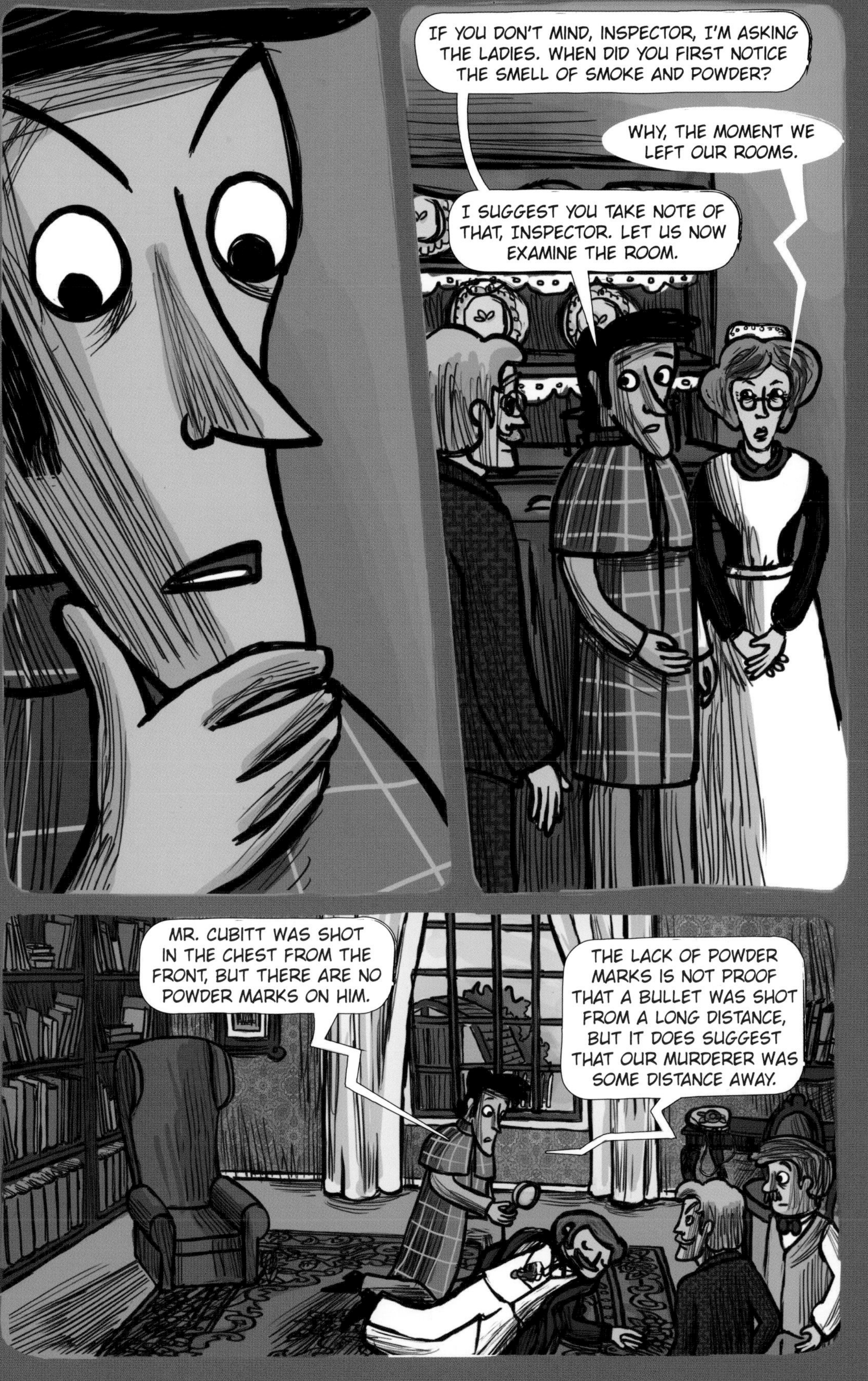
IF YOU DON'T MIND, INSPECTOR, I'M ASKING THE LADIES. WHEN DID YOU FIRST NOTICE THE SMELL OF SMOKE AND POWDER?
WHY, THE MOMENT WE LEFT OUR ROOMS.
I SUGGEST YOU TAKE NOTE OF THAT, INSPECTOR. LET US NOW EXAMINE THE ROOM.
MR. CUBITT WAS SHOT IN THE CHEST FROM THE FRONT, BUT THERE ARE NO POWDER MARKS ON HIM.
THE LACK OF POWDER MARKS IS NOT PROOF THAT A BULLET WAS SHOT FROM A LONG DISTANCE, BUT IT DOES SUGGEST THAT OUR MURDERER WAS SOME DISTANCE AWAY.

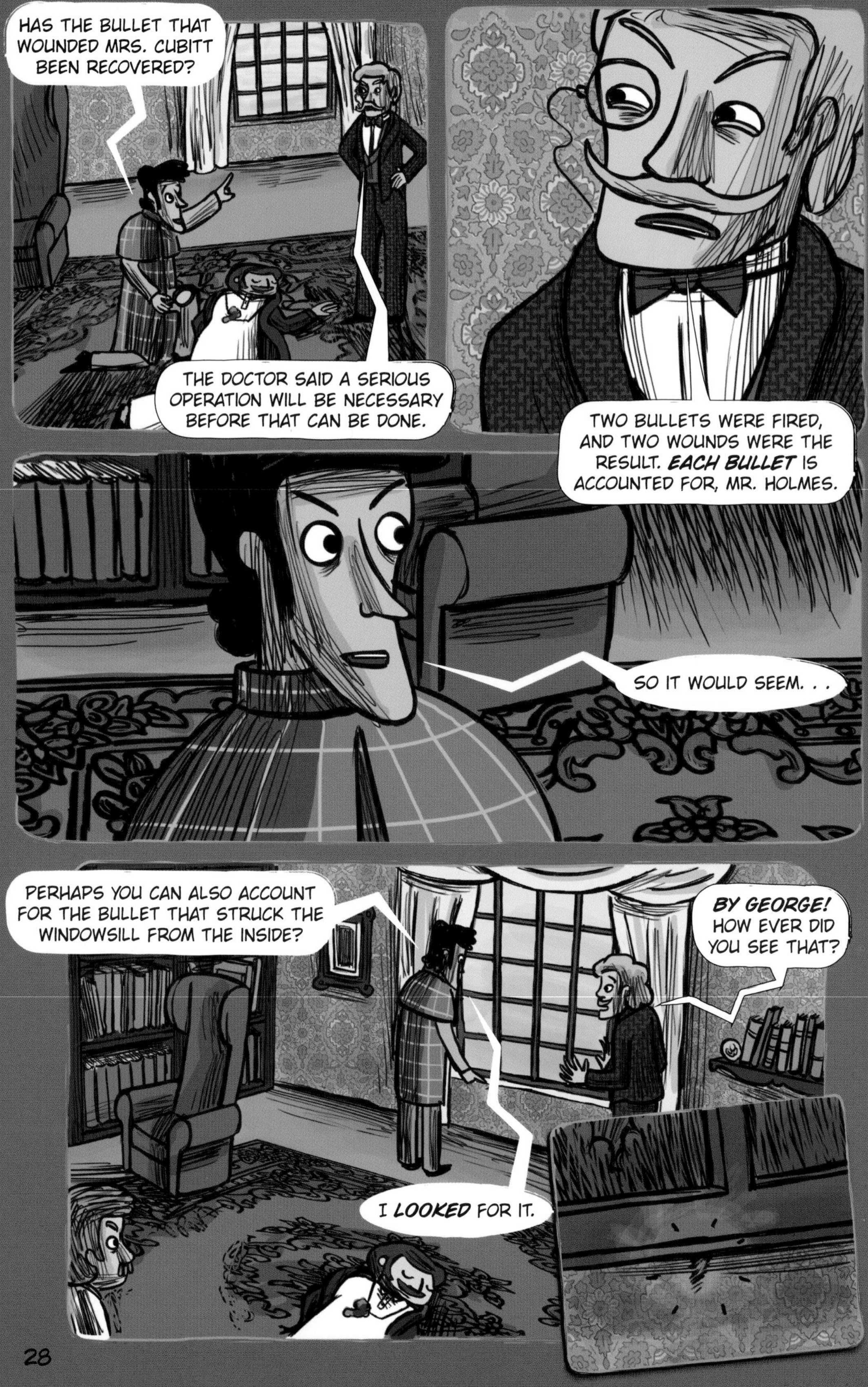
HAS THE BULLET THAT WOUNDED MRS. CUBITT BEEN RECOVERED?
THE DOCTOR SAID A SERIOUS OPERATION WILL BE NECESSARY BEFORE THAT CAN BE DONE.
TWO BULLETS WERE FIRED, AND TWO WOUNDS WERE THE RESULT. ***EACH BULLET*** IS ACCOUNTED FOR, MR. HOLMES.
SO IT WOULD SEEM. . .
PERHAPS YOU CAN ALSO ACCOUNT FOR THE BULLET THAT STRUCK THE WINDOWSILL FROM THE INSIDE?
BY GEORGE! HOW EVER DID YOU SEE THAT?
I ***LOOKED*** FOR IT.

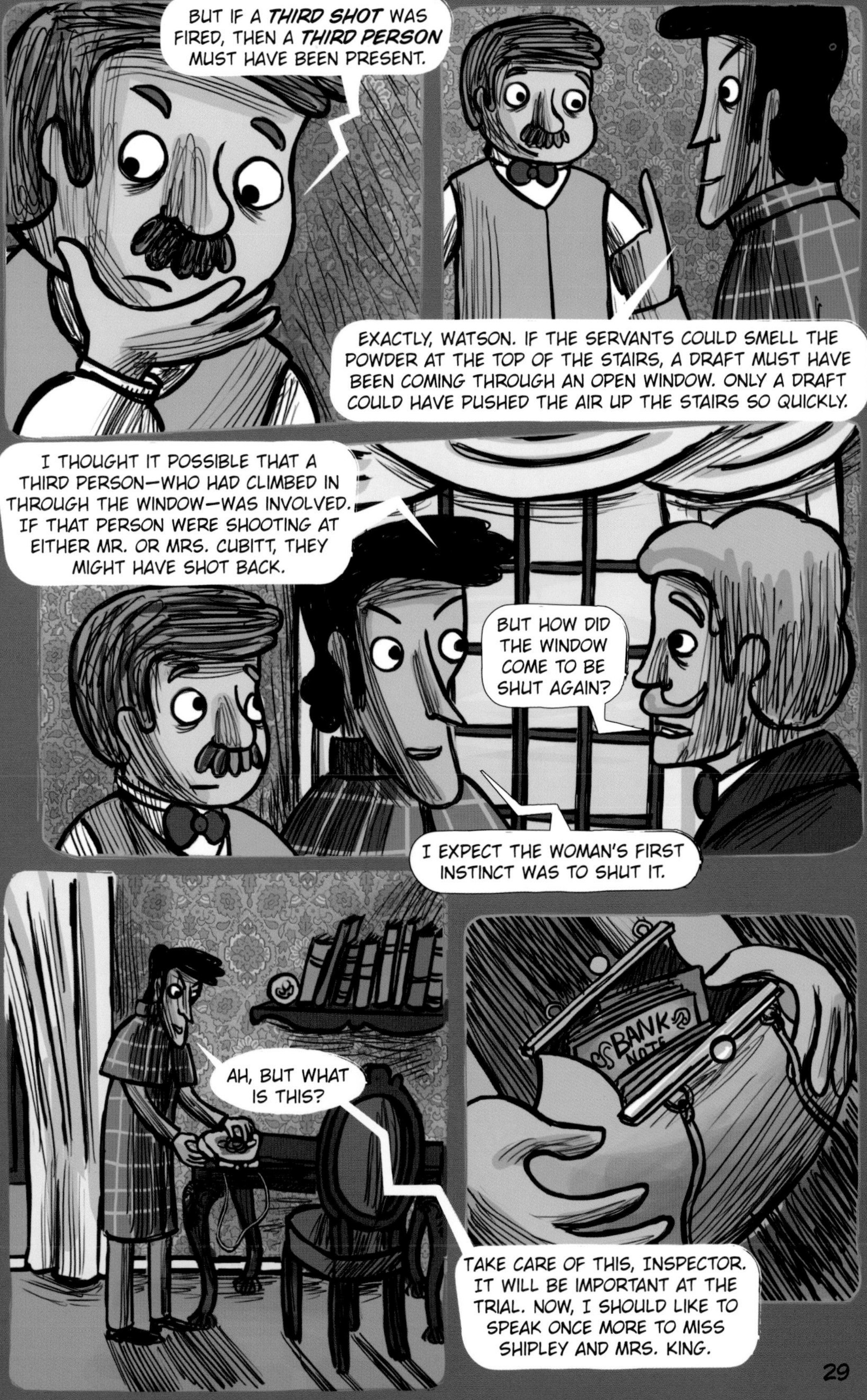
BUT IF A THIRD SHOT WAS FIRED, THEN A THIRD PERSON MUST HAVE BEEN PRESENT.
EXACTLY, WATSON. IF THE SERVANTS COULD SMELL THE POWDER AT THE TOP OF THE STAIRS, A DRAFT MUST HAVE BEEN COMING THROUGH AN OPEN WINDOW. ONLY A DRAFT COULD HAVE PUSHED THE AIR UP THE STAIRS SO QUICKLY.
I THOUGHT IT POSSIBLE THAT A THIRD PERSON—WHO HAD CLIMBED IN THROUGH THE WINDOW—WAS INVOLVED. IF THAT PERSON WERE SHOOTING AT EITHER MR. OR MRS. CUBITT, THEY MIGHT HAVE SHOT BACK.
BUT HOW DID THE WINDOW COME TO BE SHUT AGAIN?
I EXPECT THE WOMAN'S FIRST INSTINCT WAS TO SHUT IT.
AH, BUT WHAT IS THIS?
BANK NOTE
TAKE CARE OF THIS, INSPECTOR. IT WILL BE IMPORTANT AT THE TRIAL. NOW, I SHOULD LIKE TO SPEAK ONCE MORE TO MISS SHIPLEY AND MRS. KING.

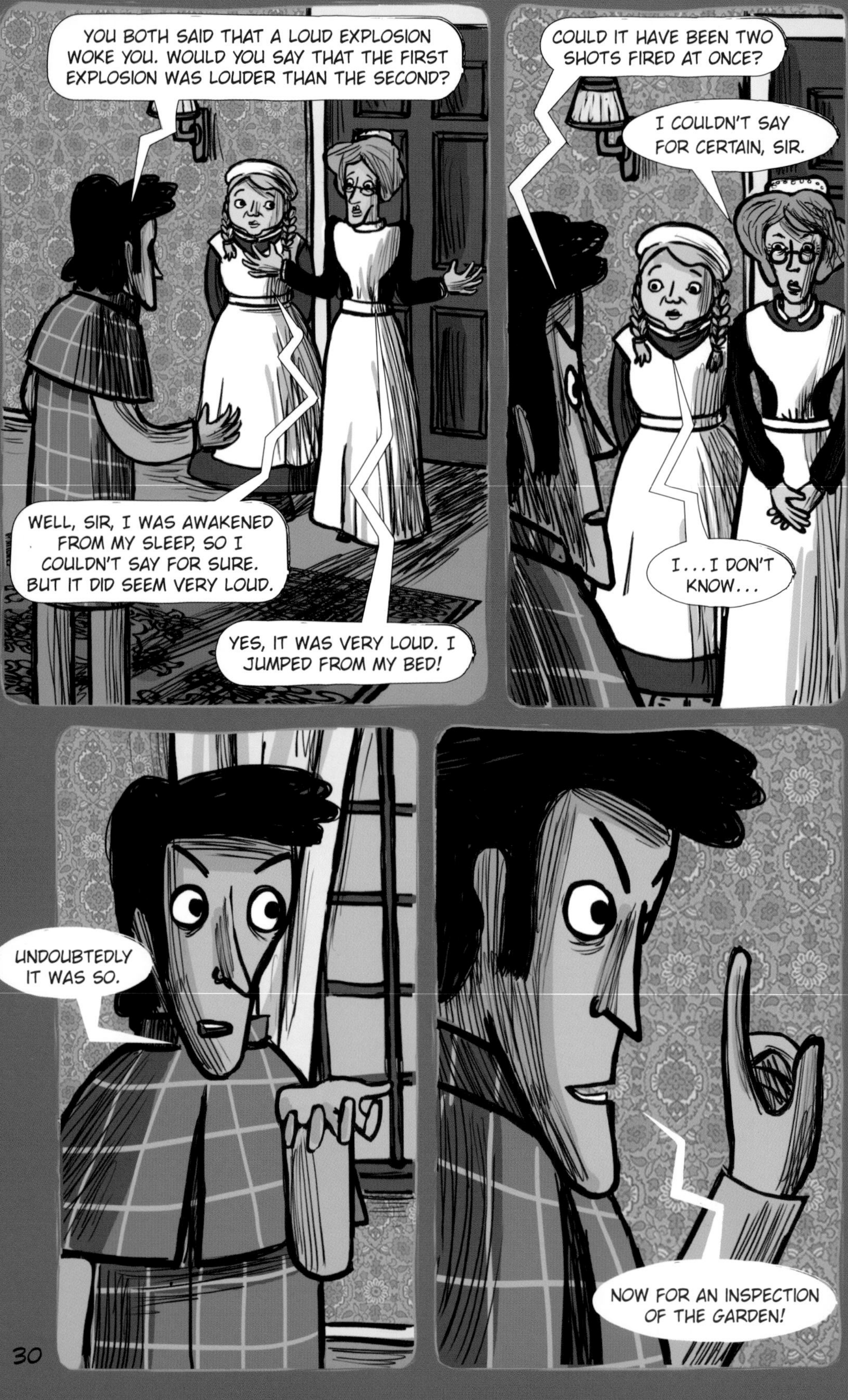
YOU BOTH SAID THAT A LOUD EXPLOSION WOKE YOU. WOULD YOU SAY THAT THE FIRST EXPLOSION WAS LOUDER THAN THE SECOND?
WELL, SIR, I WAS AWAKENED FROM MY SLEEP, SO I COULDN'T SAY FOR SURE. BUT IT DID SEEM VERY LOUD.
YES, IT WAS VERY LOUD. I JUMPED FROM MY BED!
COULD IT HAVE BEEN TWO SHOTS FIRED AT ONCE?
I COULDN'T SAY FOR CERTAIN, SIR.
I . . . I DON'T KNOW . . .
UNDOUBTEDLY IT WAS SO.
NOW FOR AN INSPECTION OF THE GARDEN!

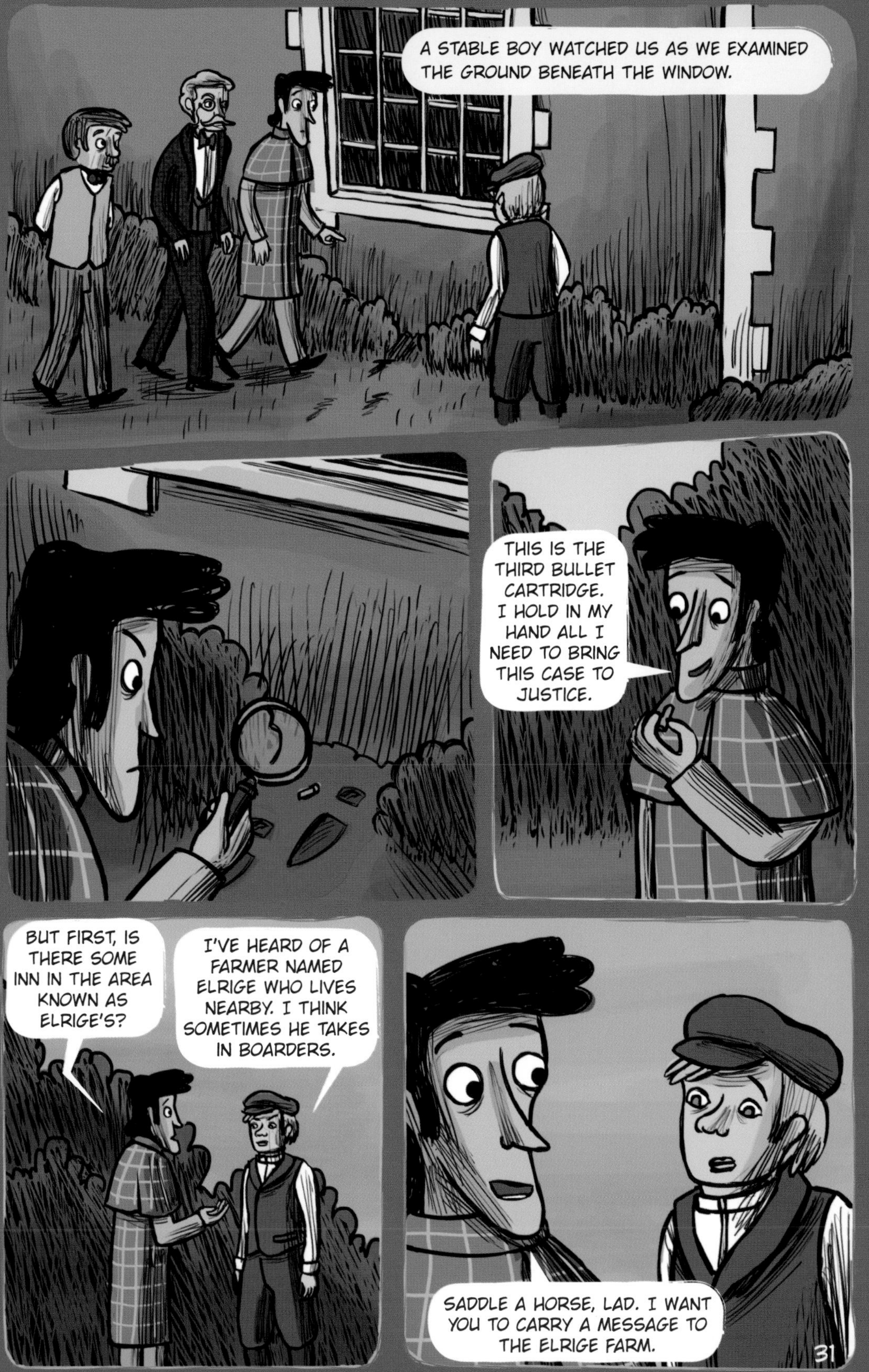
A STABLE BOY WATCHED US AS WE EXAMINED THE GROUND BENEATH THE WINDOW.
THIS IS THE THIRD BULLET CARTRIDGE. I HOLD IN MY HAND ALL I NEED TO BRING THIS CASE TO JUSTICE.
BUT FIRST, IS THERE SOME INN IN THE AREA KNOWN AS ELRIGE'S?
I'VE HEARD OF A FARMER NAMED ELRIGE WHO LIVES NEARBY. I THINK SOMETIMES HE TAKES IN BOARDERS.
SADDLE A HORSE, LAD. I WANT YOU TO CARRY A MESSAGE TO THE ELRIGE FARM.

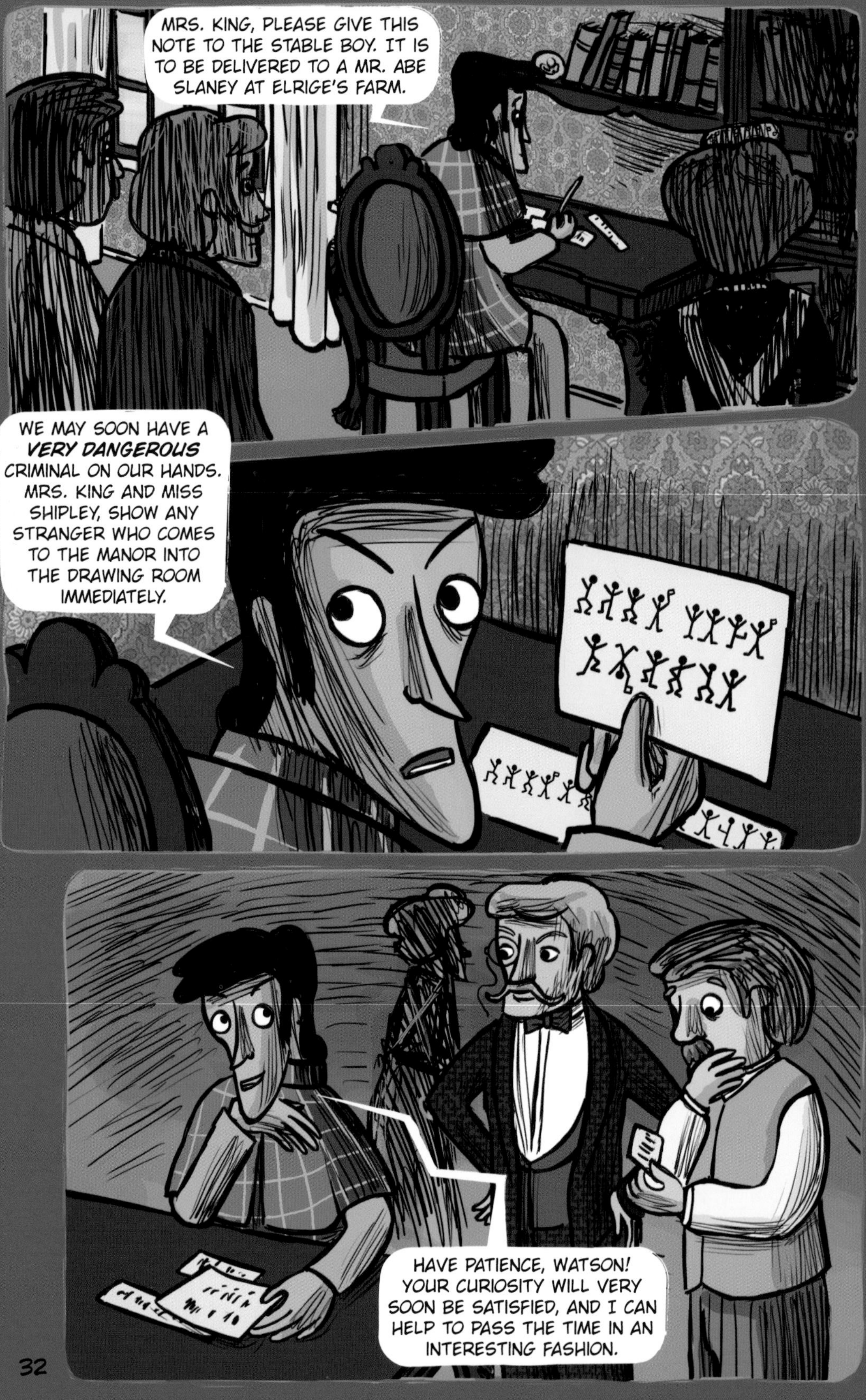
MRS. KING, PLEASE GIVE THIS NOTE TO THE STABLE BOY. IT IS TO BE DELIVERED TO A MR. ABE SLANEY AT ELRIGE'S FARM.
WE MAY SOON HAVE A ***VERY DANGEROUS*** CRIMINAL ON OUR HANDS. MRS. KING AND MISS SHIPLEY, SHOW ANY STRANGER WHO COMES TO THE MANOR INTO THE DRAWING ROOM IMMEDIATELY.
HAVE PATIENCE, WATSON! YOUR CURIOSITY WILL VERY SOON BE SATISFIED, AND I CAN HELP TO PASS THE TIME IN AN INTERESTING FASHION.

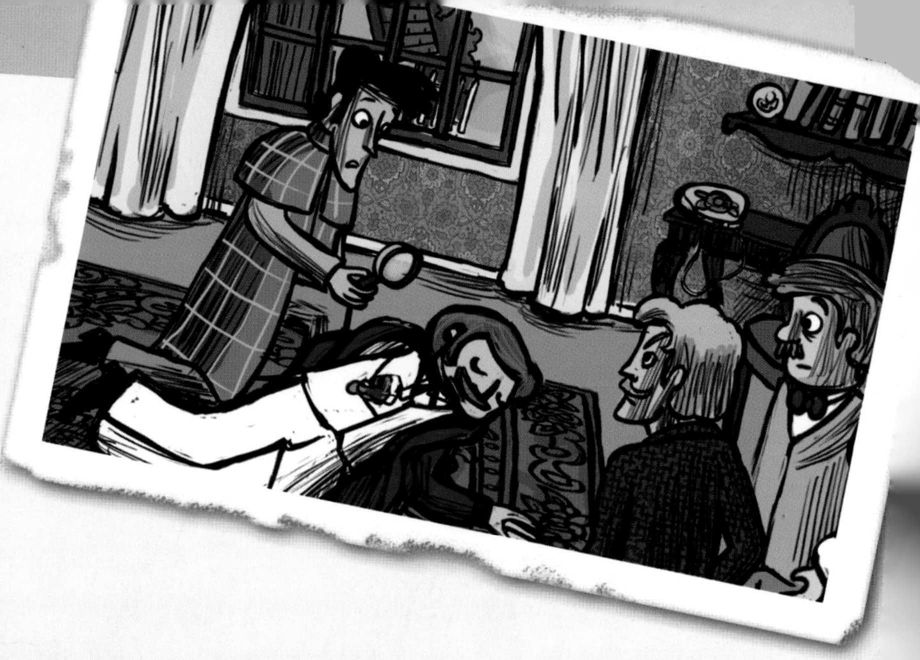

Turning to the notes on the table, Holmes showed us how he had decoded the message of the dancing men and discovered the murderer's identity. He then gave the inspector an account of the case from the beginning.

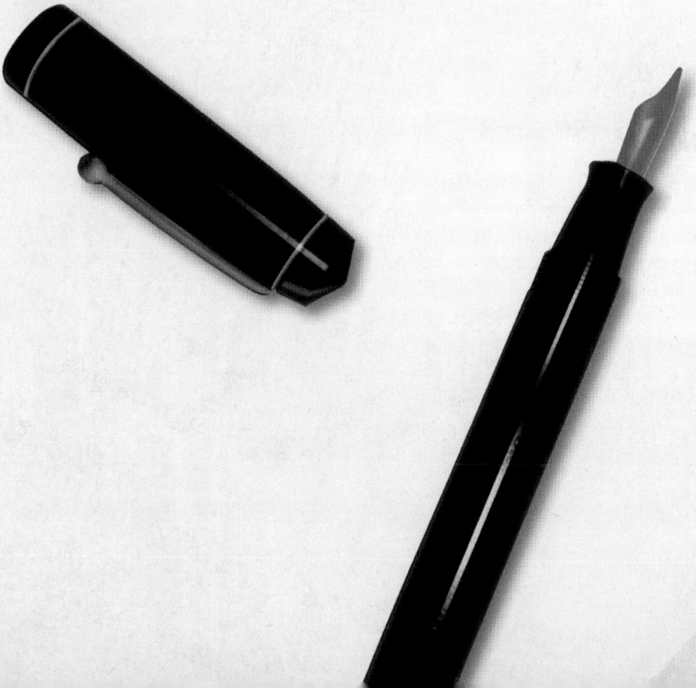

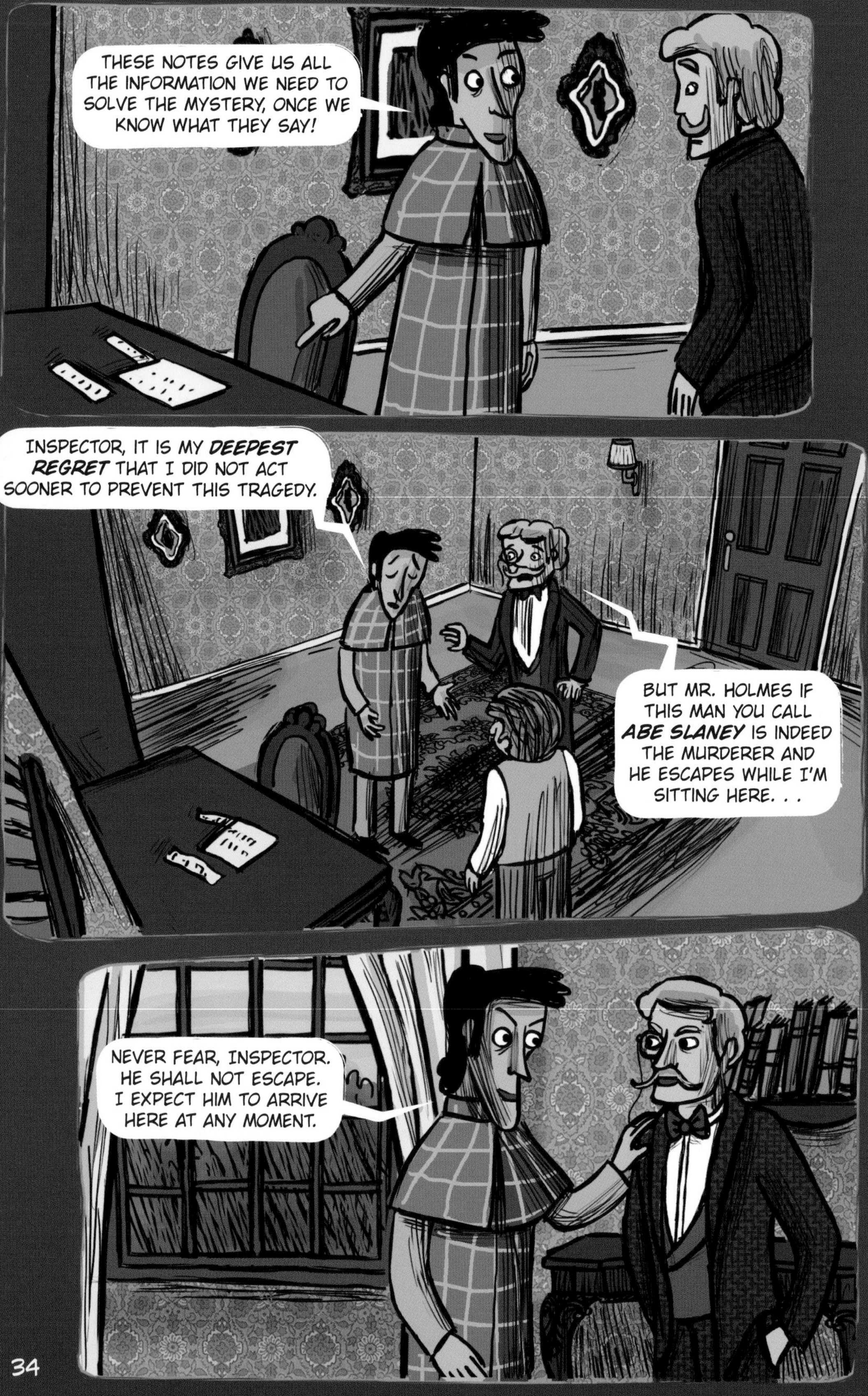
THESE NOTES GIVE US ALL THE INFORMATION WE NEED TO SOLVE THE MYSTERY, ONCE WE KNOW WHAT THEY SAY!
INSPECTOR, IT IS MY ***DEEPEST REGRET*** THAT I DID NOT ACT SOONER TO PREVENT THIS TRAGEDY.
BUT MR. HOLMES IF THIS MAN YOU CALL ***ABE SLANEY*** IS INDEED THE MURDERER AND HE ESCAPES WHILE I'M SITTING HERE. . .
NEVER FEAR, INSPECTOR. HE SHALL NOT ESCAPE. I EXPECT HIM TO ARRIVE HERE AT ANY MOMENT.

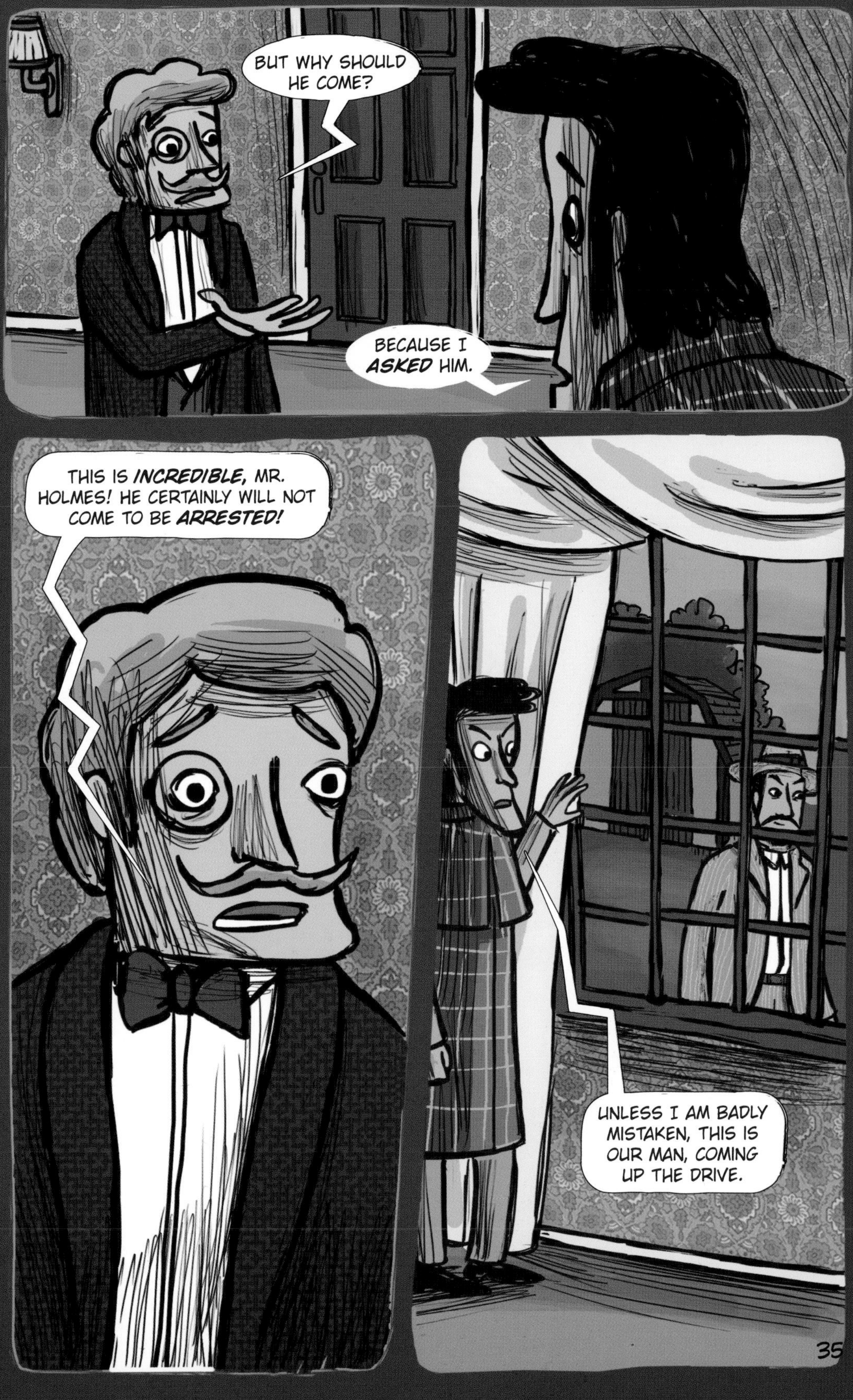
BUT WHY SHOULD HE COME?
BECAUSE I ASKED HIM.
THIS IS INCREDIBLE, MR. HOLMES! HE CERTAINLY WILL NOT COME TO BE ARRESTED!
UNLESS I AM BADLY MISTAKEN, THIS IS OUR MAN, COMING UP THE DRIVE.

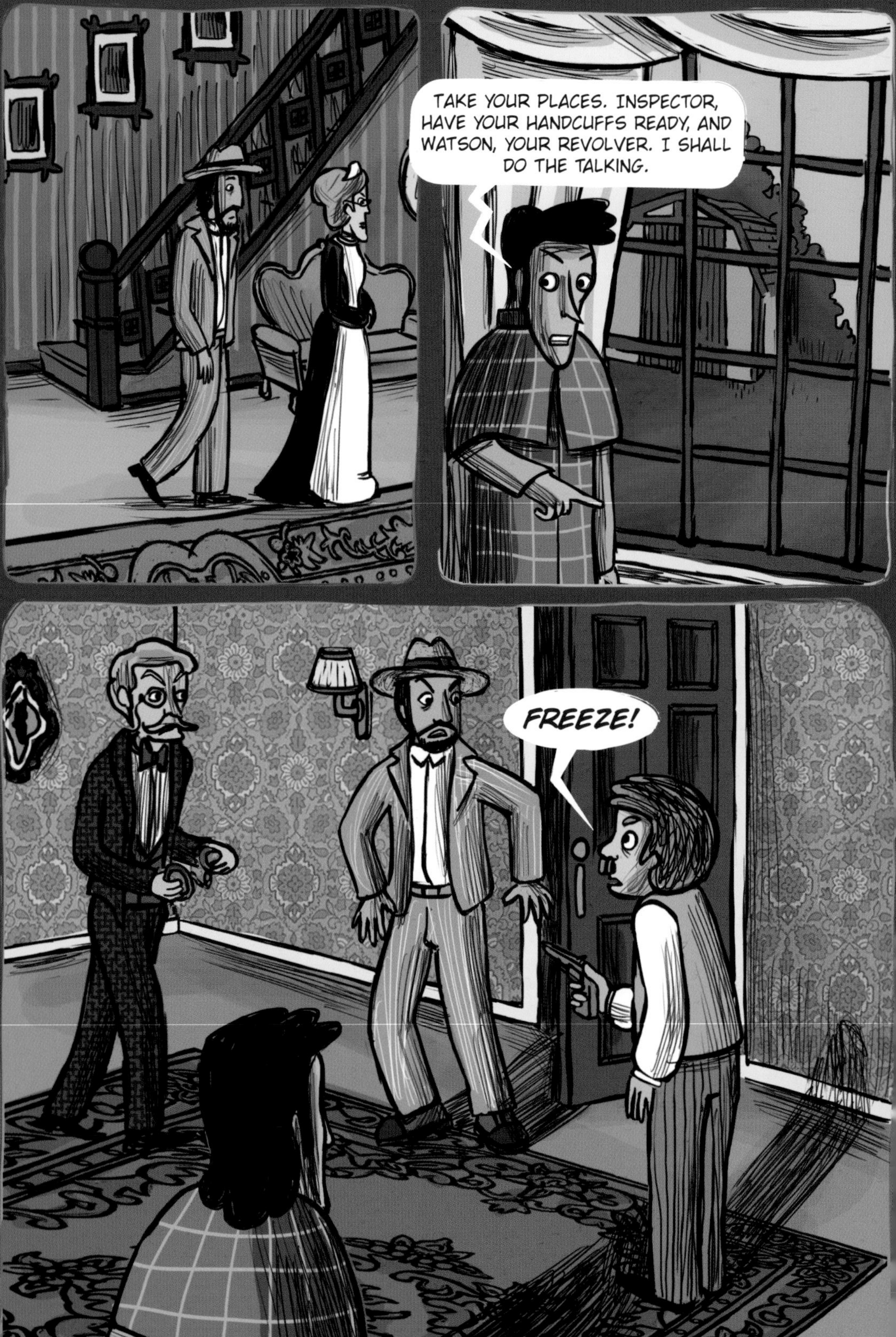
TAKE YOUR PLACES. INSPECTOR, HAVE YOUR HANDCUFFS READY, AND WATSON, YOUR REVOLVER. I SHALL DO THE TALKING.
FREEZE!

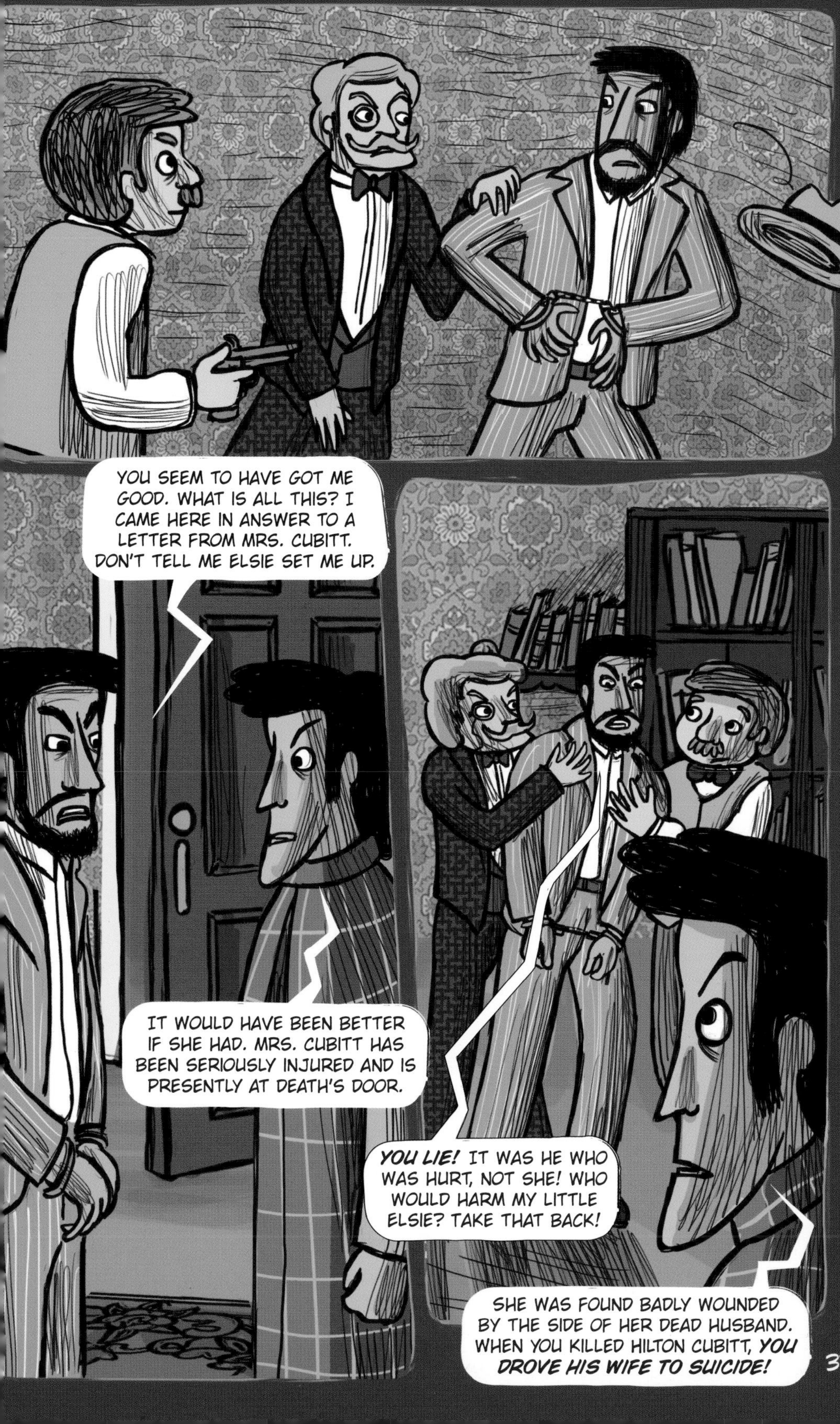
YOU SEEM TO HAVE GOT ME GOOD. WHAT IS ALL THIS? I CAME HERE IN ANSWER TO A LETTER FROM MRS. CUBITT. DON'T TELL ME ELSIE SET ME UP.
IT WOULD HAVE BEEN BETTER IF SHE HAD. MRS. CUBITT HAS BEEN SERIOUSLY INJURED AND IS PRESENTLY AT DEATH'S DOOR.
YOU LIE! IT WAS HE WHO WAS HURT, NOT SHE! WHO WOULD HARM MY LITTLE ELSIE? TAKE THAT BACK!
SHE WAS FOUND BADLY WOUNDED BY THE SIDE OF HER DEAD HUSBAND. WHEN YOU KILLED HILTON CUBITT, ***YOU DROVE HIS WIFE TO SUICIDE!***

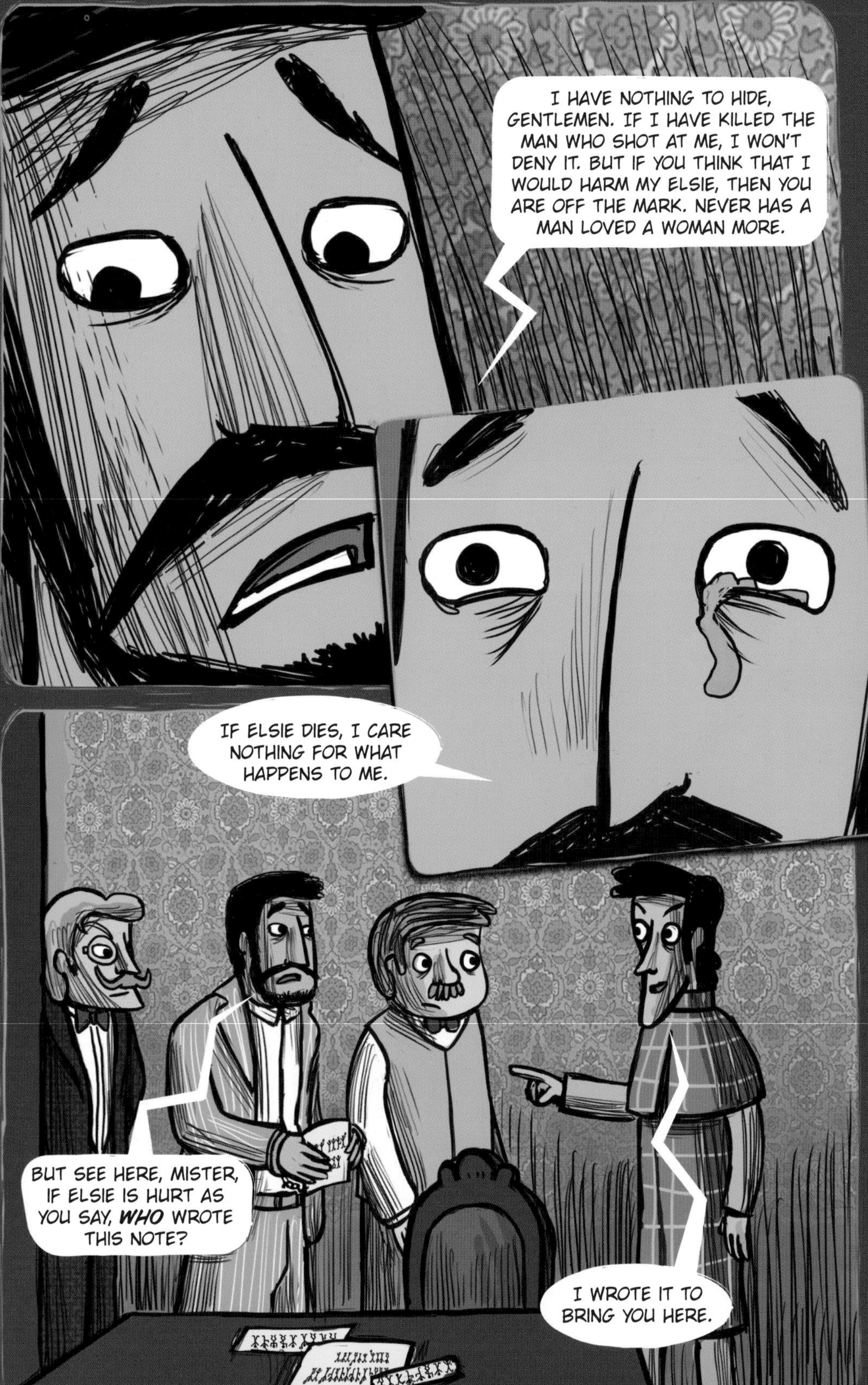
I HAVE NOTHING TO HIDE, GENTLEMEN. IF I HAVE KILLED THE MAN WHO SHOT AT ME, I WON'T DENY IT. BUT IF YOU THINK THAT I WOULD HARM MY ELSIE, THEN YOU ARE OFF THE MARK. NEVER HAS A MAN LOVED A WOMAN MORE.
IF ELSIE DIES, I CARE NOTHING FOR WHAT HAPPENS TO ME.
BUT SEE HERE, MISTER, IF ELSIE IS HURT AS YOU SAY, ***WHO*** WROTE THIS NOTE?
I WROTE IT TO BRING YOU HERE.

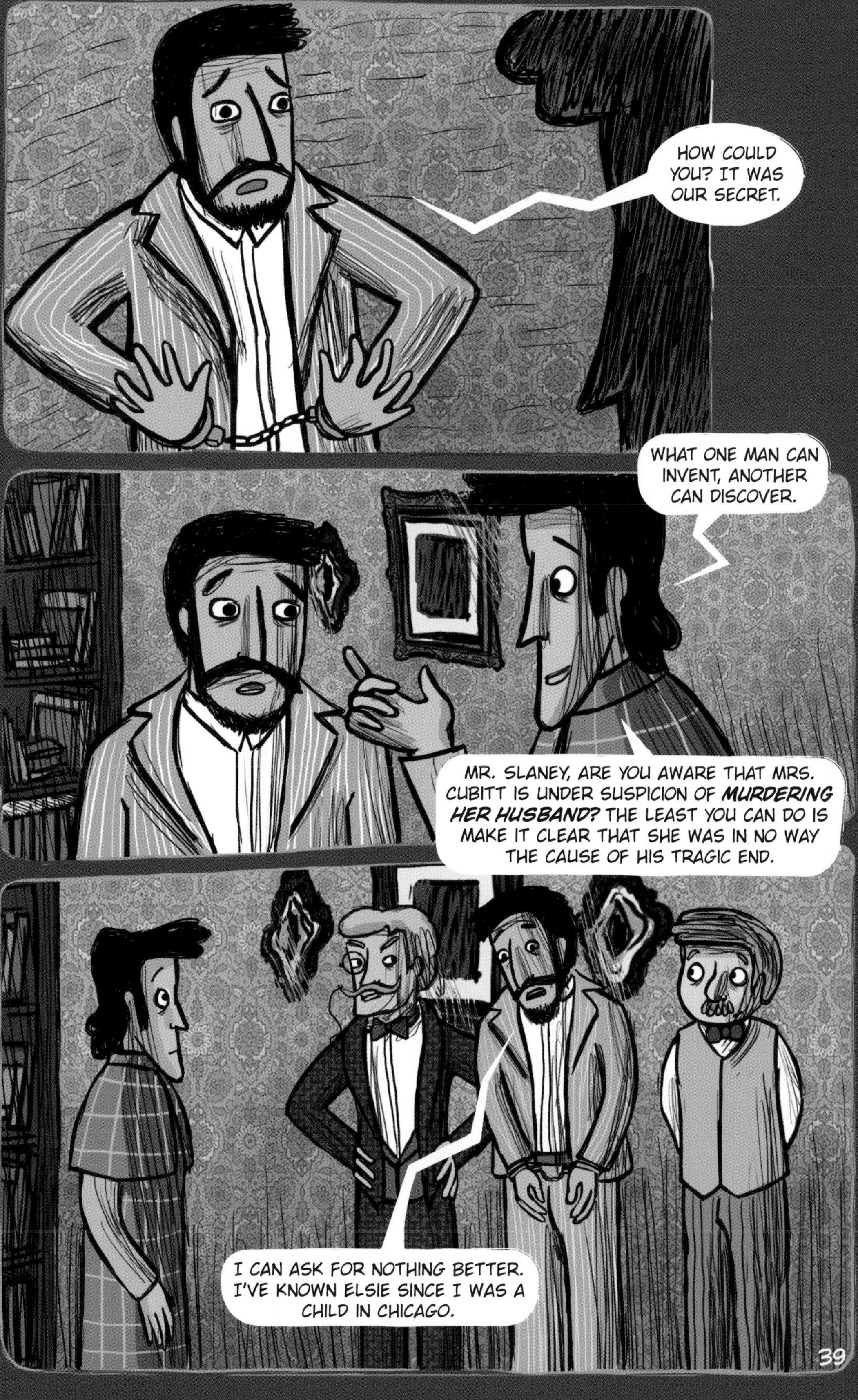
HOW COULD YOU? IT WAS OUR SECRET.
WHAT ONE MAN CAN INVENT, ANOTHER CAN DISCOVER.
MR. SLANEY, ARE YOU AWARE THAT MRS. CUBITT IS UNDER SUSPICION OF ***MURDERING HER HUSBAND?*** THE LEAST YOU CAN DO IS MAKE IT CLEAR THAT SHE WAS IN NO WAY THE CAUSE OF HIS TRAGIC END.
I CAN ASK FOR NOTHING BETTER. I'VE KNOWN ELSIE SINCE I WAS A CHILD IN CHICAGO.

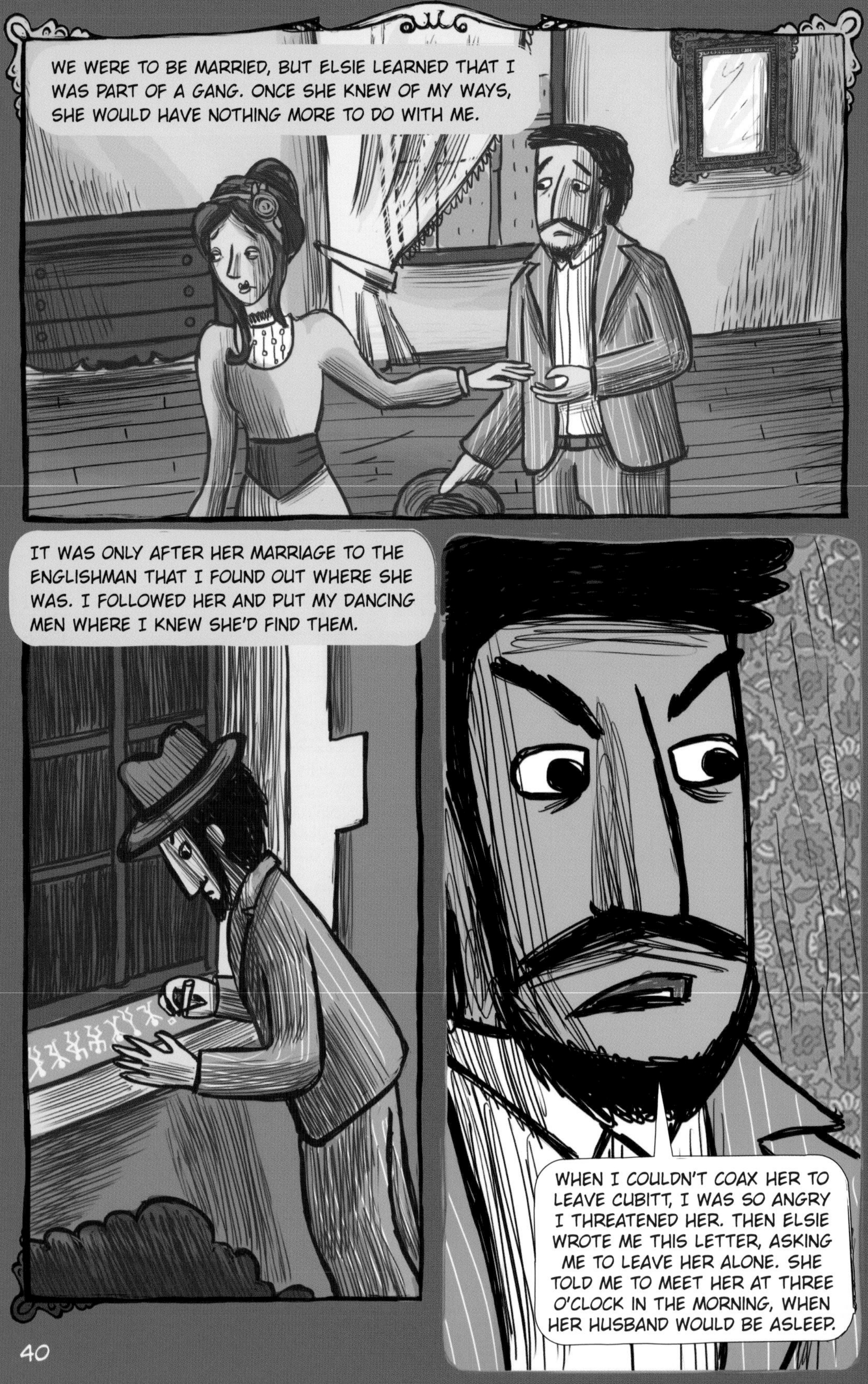
WE WERE TO BE MARRIED, BUT ELSIE LEARNED THAT I WAS PART OF A GANG. ONCE SHE KNEW OF MY WAYS, SHE WOULD HAVE NOTHING MORE TO DO WITH ME.
IT WAS ONLY AFTER HER MARRIAGE TO THE ENGLISHMAN THAT I FOUND OUT WHERE SHE WAS. I FOLLOWED HER AND PUT MY DANCING MEN WHERE I KNEW SHE'D FIND THEM.
WHEN I COULDN'T COAX HER TO LEAVE CUBITT, I WAS SO ANGRY I THREATENED HER. THEN ELSIE WROTE ME THIS LETTER, ASKING ME TO LEAVE HER ALONE. SHE TOLD ME TO MEET HER AT THREE O'CLOCK IN THE MORNING, WHEN HER HUSBAND WOULD BE ASLEEP.

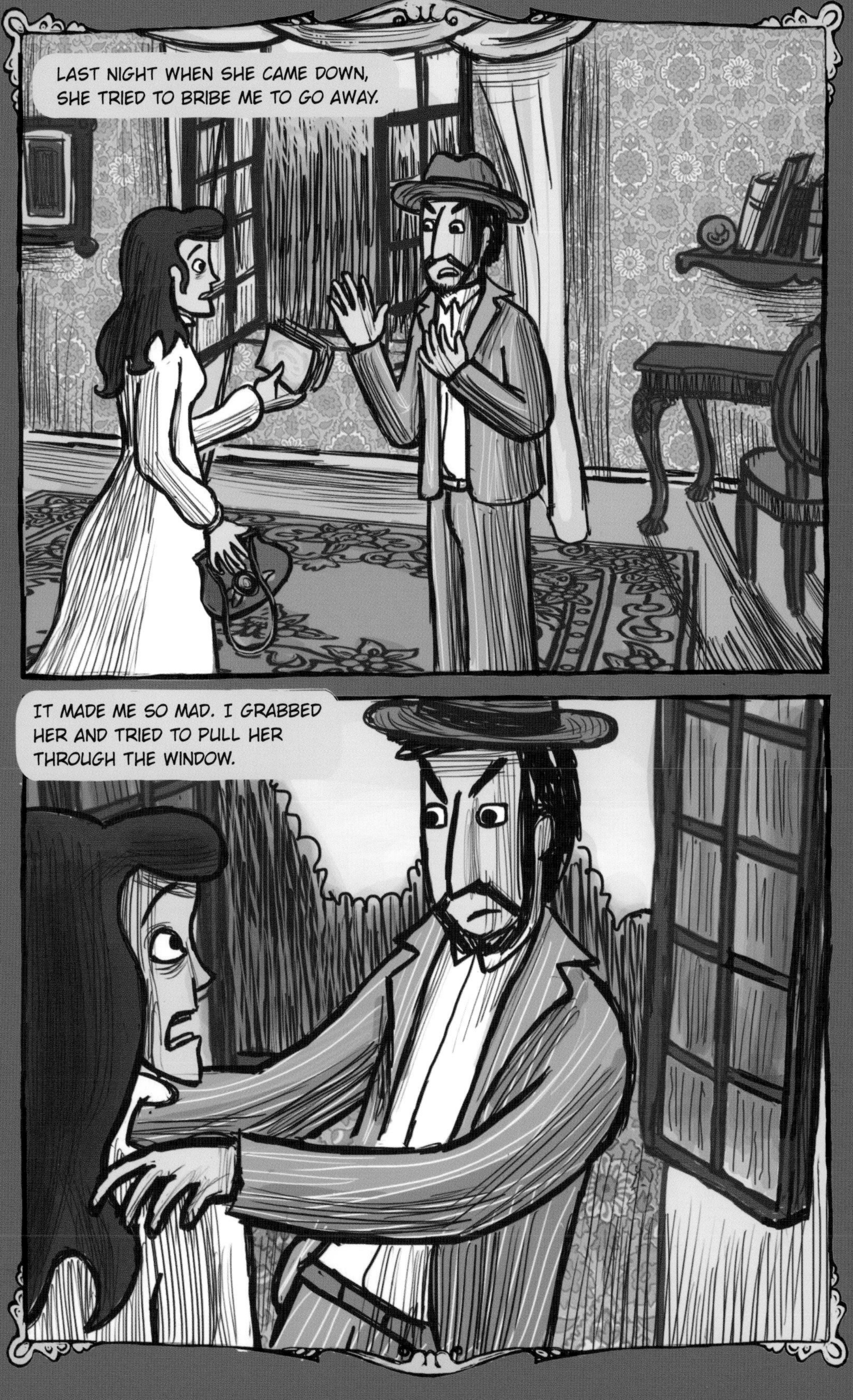
LAST NIGHT WHEN SHE CAME DOWN, SHE TRIED TO BRIBE ME TO GO AWAY.
IT MADE ME SO MAD. I GRABBED HER AND TRIED TO PULL HER THROUGH THE WINDOW.

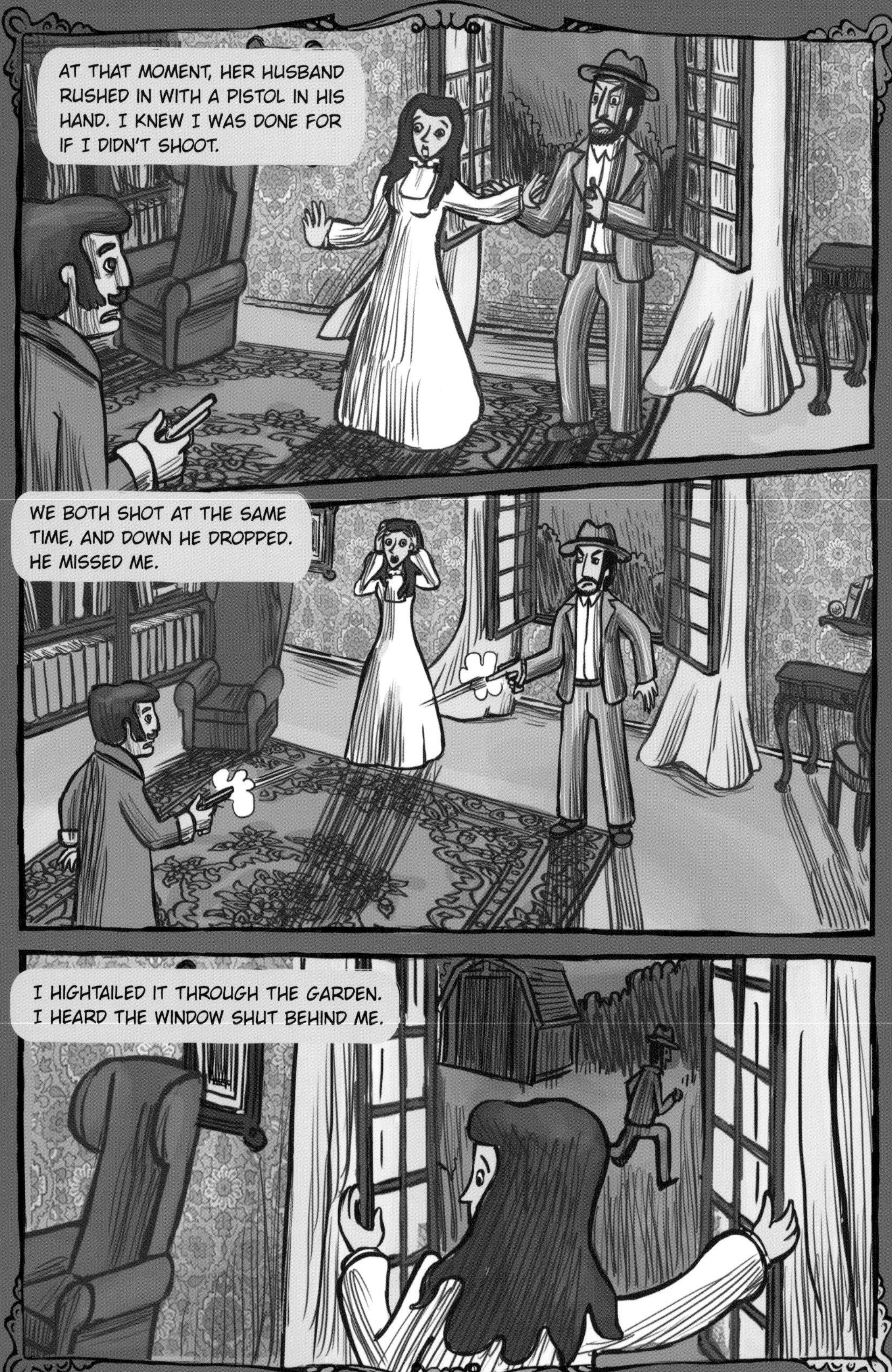
AT THAT MOMENT, HER HUSBAND RUSHED IN WITH A PISTOL IN HIS HAND. I KNEW I WAS DONE FOR IF I DIDN'T SHOOT.
WE BOTH SHOT AT THE SAME TIME, AND DOWN HE DROPPED. HE MISSED ME.
I HIGHTAILED IT THROUGH THE GARDEN. I HEARD THE WINDOW SHUT BEHIND ME.

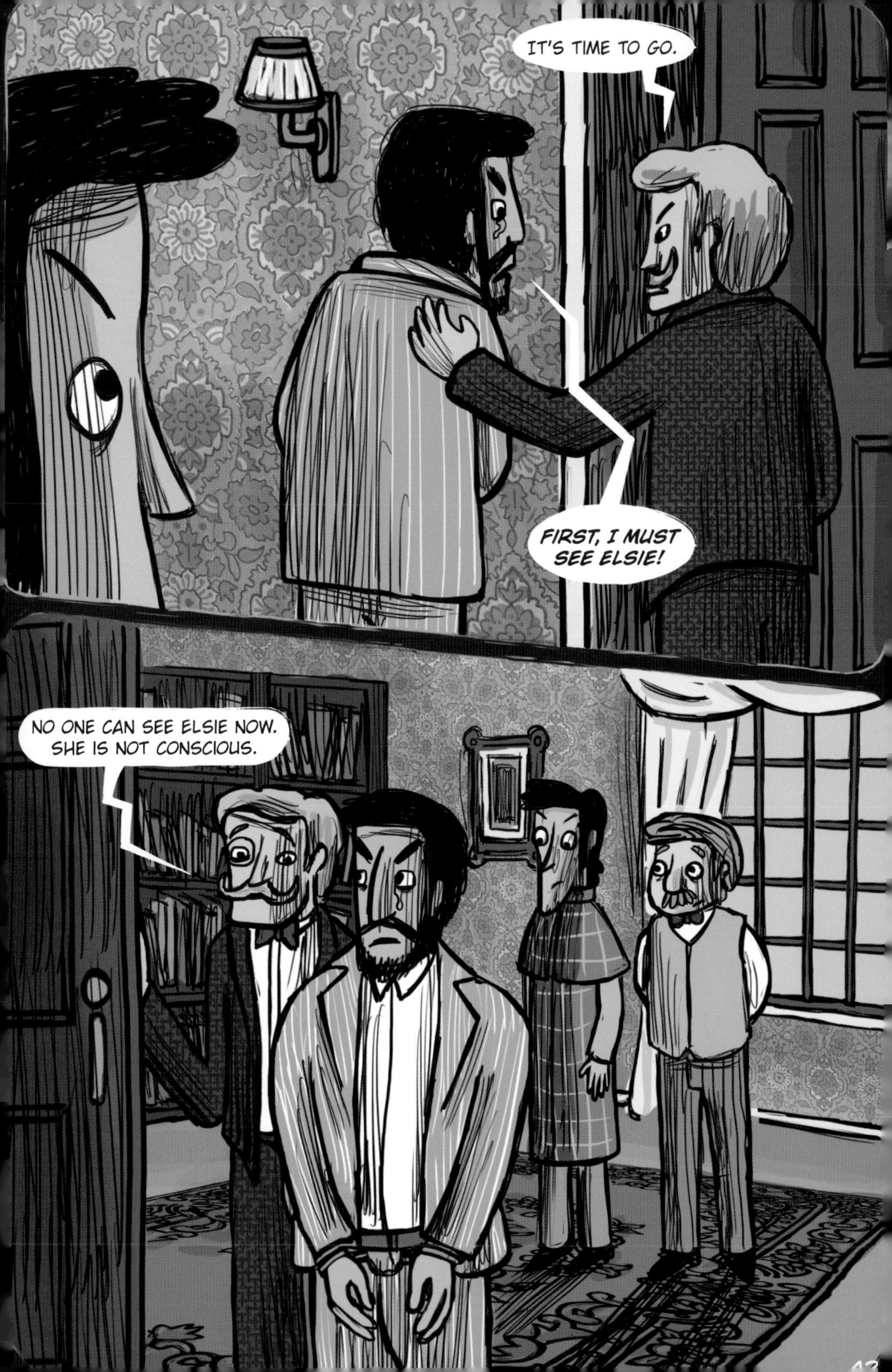
IT'S TIME TO GO.
FIRST, I MUST SEE ELSIE!
NO ONE CAN SEE ELSIE NOW. SHE IS NOT CONSCIOUS.

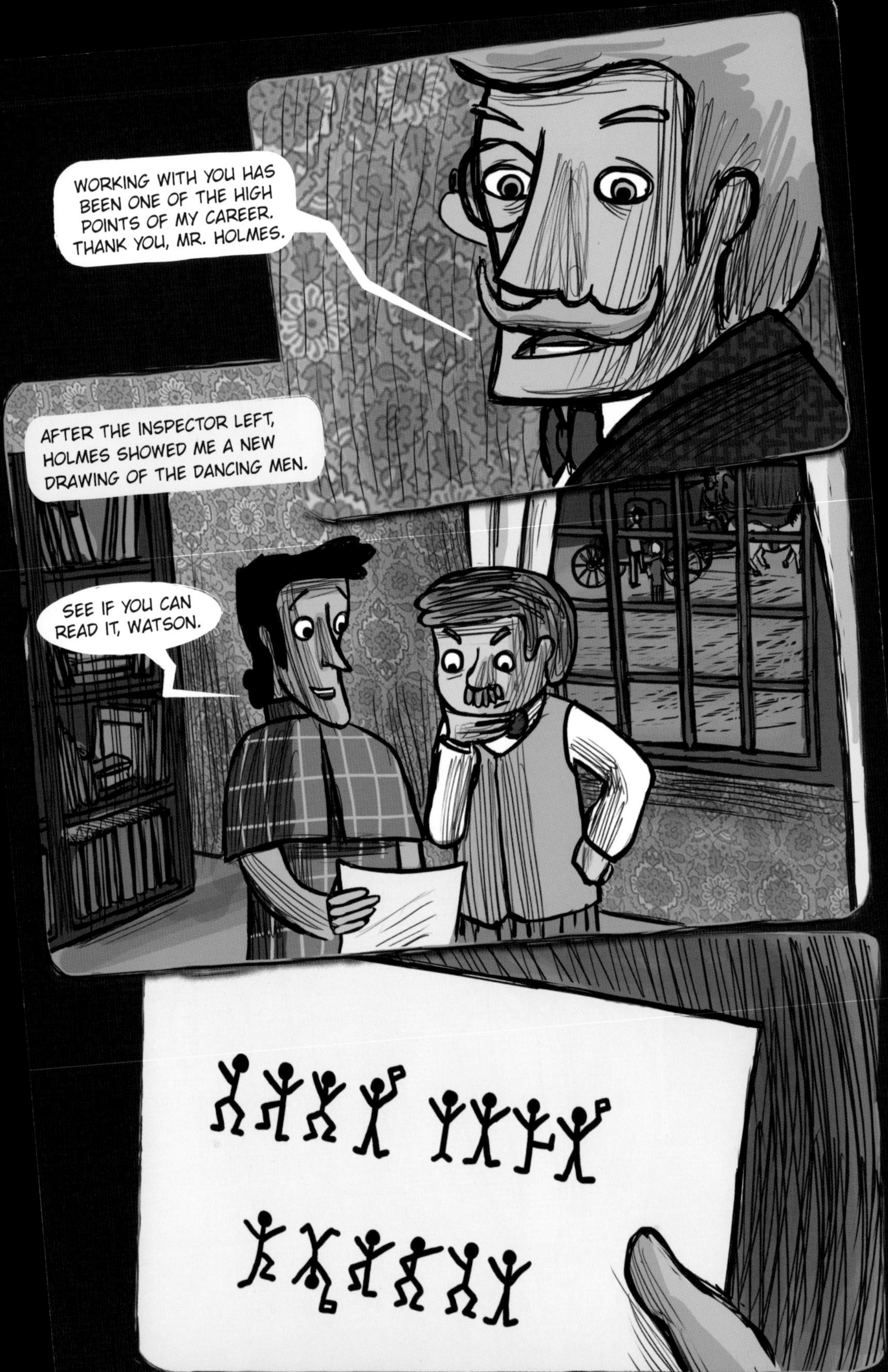
WORKING WITH YOU HAS BEEN ONE OF THE HIGH POINTS OF MY CAREER. THANK YOU, MR. HOLMES.
AFTER THE INSPECTOR LEFT, HOLMES SHOWED ME A NEW DRAWING OF THE DANCING MEN.
SEE IF YOU CAN READ IT, WATSON.

The slip contained nothing but a line of dancing men. But this time, using Holmes's method of decoding, I was able to read the message: "Come here at once." After I finished, my dear and brilliant friend said, "You see, Watson, every problem becomes quite simple once it is explained."

From the Desk of
John H. Watson, M.D.

The Adventure of the Dancing Men: How Did Holmes Solve It?

How did Holmes crack the code?

Holmes was a master at decoding messages. Holmes felt confident that the symbol  stood for an *E*, because *E* is the most common letter in the English language. This symbol came up four times in the message. Holmes suspected that the flags the men held indicated the ends of words.

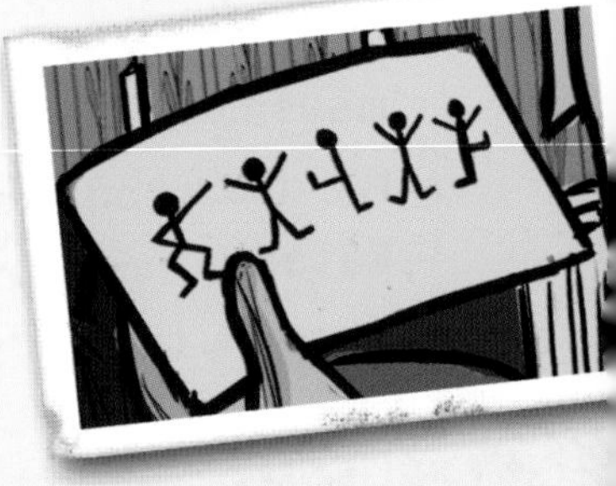

Later, Mr. Cubitt gave Holmes three more messages. One that was found on the toolshed had two *E*s: *_E_E_*. Since the most probable one-word reply to a message would be *never*, the symbols 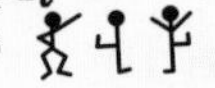 had to stand for *N*, *V*, and *R*.

Another message contained a word beginning and ending in E. Holmes thought that whoever sent the messages to Mrs. Cubitt might use her first name: Elsie. This gave Holmes the symbols for *L*, *S*, and *I*. In the same message, there was only one other word. Holmes imagined that it was a command. Since the four-letter word ended in *E*, *come* was the only word Holmes could think of to fit. Now he knew the symbols for *C*, *O*, and *M*.

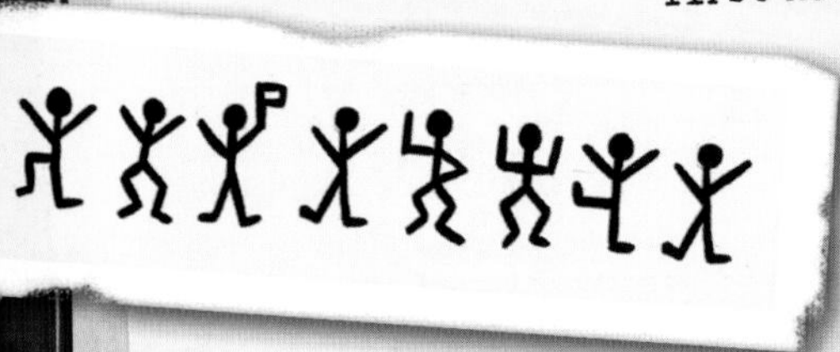

Holmes went back to the very first message. He decoded the letters he knew: "*_M_ERE _ _E SL_NE_*." The first letter could only be *A*. Knowing this, the H was easy to figure out. Now the message read, **"AM HERE A_E SLANE_."** Using common sense, Holmes finished the message: **Am Here. Abe Slaney.**

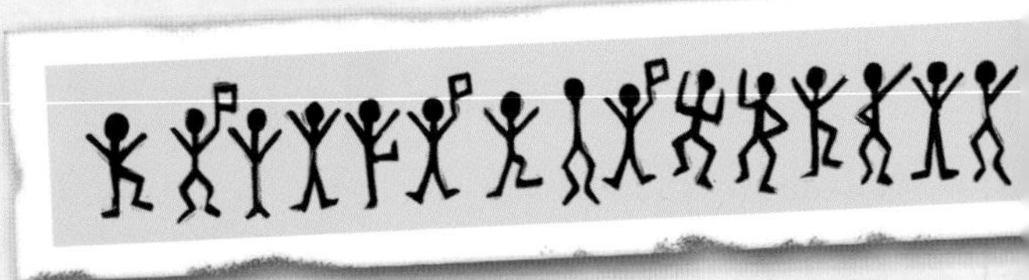

Then Holmes applied what he had learned to the first message copied down from the toolshed door. It now read, **"A_ ELRI_ES."** The only logical solution turned out to be **At Elrige's.**

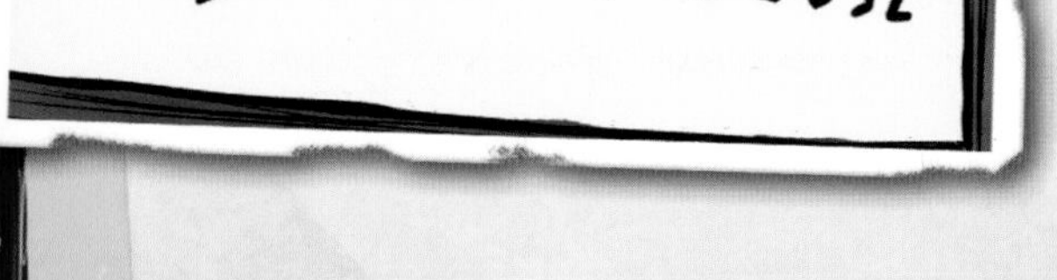

How did Holmes know Abe Slaney was dangerous?

Holmes cabled the New York Police Department to find any criminal records on Abe Slaney. They sent this message back to Holmes: "The most dangerous crook in Chicago."

In the meantime, Hilton Cubitt had found yet another message on the sundial and sent it to Holmes. Using the letters already decoded, Holmes read, "ELSIE _RE_ARE TO MEET THY GO_." Holmes filled in the blanks: Elsie, prepare to meet thy God. Holmes quickly made arrangements to go to Riding Thorpe Manor. But he was too late.

How did Holmes get Slaney to the manor?

To lure Slaney to the manor, Holmes wrote him a note. Watson used the code to read the note. Can you read the message too? After decoding the message—Come here at once—you can see why Abe Slaney came to the manor so quickly and confidently.

Further Reading and Websites

Blackwood, Gary. *Mysterious Messages: A History of Codes and Ciphers.* New York: Dutton Children's Books, 2009.

CIA Break the Code
https://www.cia.gov/kids-page/games/break-the-code/index.html

Langley, Andrew. *Codes and Code-Breaking.* London: Franklin Watts, 2009.

Levy, Janey. *Breaking the Code with Cryptography.* New York: Rosen Publishing, 2005.

Schimmel, David. *Sherlock Holmes Activity Book.* New York: Dover Publications, 2009.

Sherlock Holmes Museum
http://www.sherlock-holmes.co.uk

Singh, Simon. *The Code Book: How to Make It, Break It, Hack It, Crack It.* New York: Delacorte Press, 2003.

221 Baker Street
http://221bakerstreet.org

About the Author

Sir Arthur Conan Doyle was born on May 22, 1859. He became a doctor in 1882. When this career did not prove successful, Doyle started writing stories. In addition to the popular Sherlock Holmes short stories and novels, Doyle also wrote historical novels, romances, and plays.

About the Adapters

Murray Shaw's lifelong passion for Sherlock Holmes began when he was a child. He was the author of the Match Wits with Sherlock Holmes series published in the 1990s. For decades, he was a popular speaker in public schools and libraries on the adventures of Holmes and Watson.

M. J. Cosson is the author of more than fifty books, both fiction and nonfiction, for children and young adults. She has long been a fan of mysteries and especially of the great detective, Sherlock Holmes. In fact, she has participated in the production of several Sherlock Holmes plays. A native of Iowa, Cosson lives in the Texas Hill Country with her husband, dogs, and cat.

About the Illustrator

French artist Sophie Rohrbach began her career after graduating in display design at the Chambre des Commerce. She went on to design displays in many top department stores including Galeries Lafayette. She also studied illustration at Emile Cohl school in Lyon, France, where she now lives with her daughter. Rohrbach has illustrated many children's books. She is passionate about the colors and patterns that she uses in her illustrations.